ENTICED BY A REAL HITTA

L. RENEE

D1522572

Enticed by a Real Hitta
Copyright 2019 by L. Renee

Published by Mz. Lady P Presents

1

LOUVE

The splash of the water as hit the shore was all that could be heard other than the birds and the cars as they passed by us. I'm waiting for the perfect moment to tell Kilo I'm pregnant, but he just lost his job, and we are facing eviction for the fourth time, so I'm stuck contemplating what to do. My heart wants this baby after we lost the last one a few months ago. The struggles we are facing are enough to make anyone fold. I try to be his peace, be uplifting, and help keep him on the straight and narrow, but sitting here watching him I know what he is thinking. I know him all too well.

"Bae, I know things are real hard right now, but I need you to stay positive someway somehow," I said as I moved closer and rested my head on his shoulder.

We were at The Overlook just relaxing and clearing our heads like we do, but mostly avoiding the property manager until she left for the day.

"There ain't shit positive about being a black man right now, Louve. I changed for you and us, and with how I'm feeling right now, I feel like that was a mistake. I was making moves and stacking money more money than I knew what to do with. That brief run-in with them niggas out east had me seeing it had to be more to life for our three kids and us. So I changed but fuck, we broke, I got laid off for the third time, and my back is against the wall. We are about to be sleeping on the streets if I don't make these moves," he replied as he tossed a rock off the cliff.

I was speechless because he really made the choice to go back to the streets after almost losing his life. I was always willing to ride and hold my man down, but when would he really ride for me and not the streets?

"Kilo, I'm pregnant, and I'm keeping my baby. Now I know you don't like me to step in and help out, but FUCK that. I'm calling my brother like I should have done two weeks ago when you lost your job. He will front us some money, and if you would just put your pride aside, he has a job for you at his dealership," I pleaded damn near on the verge of tears.

I stood to my feet and stood directly in front of Kilo. I needed him to look me in my eyes and connect with me. We had to figure this out without the streets. I almost lost him once, and I can't lose him now.

"We can't FUCKING afford another kid, Louve! We barely can feed our damn selves let alone another baby. Fuck, man! See, this is the shit I'm talking about. I got to make these moves man, and it's funny that you mention your brother. You praise that man and think he is God's gift to everyone. Well, he ain't. He's the nigga in these streets, and that dealership is a front, ma. He's the one that I'm about to make these moves for. That job he wanted me to take is to be his distro!" he shouted as he glared over at me fist balled tightly. Kilo jumped up and stormed off to the truck leaving me stuck on stupid.

You think you know someone and then you find out that you don't know them at all. My brother Edge had some explaining to do. How could he be the plug and participate in the very same shit that destroyed our family? My father was facing football numbers behind drugs, and our mother was somewhere strung out on them. Why would Edge do that after witnessing the way drugs destroyed our family from both ends of the stick? On top of that, he lied to me all this time and most importantly, why did he have to pull Kilo into it knowing how I feel about it. Kilo has a family that he needs to come home to at night not just himself, and in the game, that isn't always a guarantee.

Kilo had me all kinds of fucked up if he thought I was about to sit back and be Bonnie to the bullshit in these streets. This is only going to bring more drama and stress our way. All money ain't good money, and fast money doesn't last long. With the responsibility of being a distro or supplier, along with it came late nights, long days, enemies, haters, and hoes. I was already unmarried with three kids and a fourth on the way. God forbid something happens then I'm just left out here to raise these kids alone with no stability. I was supposed to be a makeup artist living the life. At twenty-six, I was far from my dreams and at this point, I had given up on them. Kilo wanted his woman at home, and he wanted to be the sole provider. Me being young and dumb, I fell for it.

I met Kilo my senior year of high school at a house party I went to with my crew Sherai and Tori. We were best friends since middle school in Long Beach. Sherai moved to Cali after some tragic incident with her mother's boyfriend and her brother. Apparently, her mother's boyfriend was molesting her and about to rape her when her brother caught him and killed him. He shot him dead in her bedroom, which sent her brother to jail and her here with her aunt and uncle who adopted her after they fought to get her out of the foster care system.

Tori was born and raised in Cali and was a true west coast chick at heart. I loved her though. She had a carefree spirit, and she was the one to bring us all together one day when these older chicks from our old neighborhood tried to jump for my new Chuck Taylors. We have been thick as thieves since that day. Tori was the oldest of us and the oldest of her siblings, so she was like the mother to us all. With me being raised by my dad and brother, I yearned for a mother or even a sister, and they filled that gap. We did everything together, including going to our first house party.

I finally made my way to the truck where Kilo was smoking on a blunt bopping his head to Tupac's "California Love". I got in, buckled my seatbelt, and didn't say one word to Kilo. I threw on my shades even though the sun had set a long time ago, and the sky was almost black. I was tired, and I didn't want to talk or look at Kilo right now. We rode over Edge's home to pick up our kids Kilandre Jr. a.k.a KJ, Kiloni, and Kilai. Our son was the oldest at eight, Kiloni was six, and Kailis was four. It wasn't easy being a young mother and raising three kids, but I wouldn't change it for the world. I loved my babies. Edge's fiancée was my girl Tori, who I had a bone to pick with her as well because I know for a fact that she has to know what Edge is into.

They both were some sneaky ass people, and I knew that so why was I surprised they were still keeping secrets eight years later. Tori and Edge hid they relationship my whole pregnancy with KJ because they were afraid that I'd be upset. I mean it was weird, but Tori had lusted over Edge since middle school and with her being a year older, it was no surprise that she wanted an older man. I found out when she was supposed to be away visiting her family in Chicago, but instead, I found her ass up face down in Edge's living room when I crashed over there after a fight with Kilo. Tori apologized for months, and I made her make it up by taking me to get my hair and nails done, and ever since, she's been my sister like always.

When Sherai left Cali to go to Atlanta to mend her relationship with her brother after he was released from prison, she had become distant and only called us once in a while, so all I really had was Tori outside of Kilo and Edge. Tori had the kids for us like always because she was the godmotherzilla from hell. I couldn't do anything without her unless I wanted to fight. It was cool they loved they Auntie Tori, and Edge was loving having the kids around in hopes that Tori would be ready for a baby soon. Tori was a real estate agent and also an interior decorator, and she played no games about her business and money, so Edge was gone have to sneak that baby in on her.

2

LOUVE

I let my mind wander about Kilo and my relationship and my thoughts took me back to when it all started nine years ago. I could remember the exact day like it was yesterday.

It was the start of my senior year, and nobody could tell my girls and me a damn thing. We all had jobs and our own money, and we stayed fly every day of the week. August in Cali was a scorcher, but we were used to it by now. The first party of the year was tonight, the first Friday of many, and I was ready to see what these parties were all about. My brother would never let me go before, but now that he moved out and was busy with his car dealership, I was able to do a lot more. Tori had just purchased her first car— a used 2004 Dodge Stratus, which wasn't bad considering it was 2008. We had planned our outfits weeks ago, and all we had to do was our hair and makeup. Makeup was my specialty, so I had us on that and Sherai was really good with hair, and she always did ours for us.

I was newly single after dumping my boyfriend Drew last week. He was a wannabe player and called himself dating the school hoe Mallory and me at the same time. He barely had a chance with me, but he begged and followed me for damn near a year before I even went on a date with him. He did everything for me, and I hadn't even lost my virginity to him, and I was glad I hadn't since he turned out to be a cornball. He usually took me out every Friday since I worked on Saturday nights and Sundays but no more of those boring nights for me, I was officially done with him. I was ready to be in the mix of the parties that I always hear about. Tori had gone to a few with her cousins and some of the cheerleaders from the cheer squad she was on. According to Tori, once I went and experienced the hood niggas and the way they kick it, I'll never want to miss another one.

I had just got my hair done in some micro braids last week, so all I had to do was shower get dressed before Tori arrived. I showered and handled all my hygiene and applied some MAC Oh Baby lip gloss and nothing else because I wasn't into all that makeup stuff. I decided on some cute fitted Jordache jeans and a tight all white baby tee with the word Pretty across the front in gold letters that showed a little of my stomach and my cute diamond butterfly belly ring. I put my big gold hoops on and my bangle bracelets. I opted for my all white Adidas Samoa. I decided on wearing my Coach wristlet instead of an actual purse. I sprayed on my Tommy Girl perfume and grabbed my phone before heading out of my room.

I got downstairs and ran into my father Edmond and his right hand man, my godfather Vern. Vern and my father were thick as thieves since kids, and they met my mother Loucille and Aunt Zoe together marrying them and having families. My Aunt Zoe and Uncle Vern had three kids, Lil Vern, Vera, and Venus. I was older than the girls were by four and five years, but Lil Vern was a year older than I was. I gave Uncle Vern and my pops a hug before heading to the kitchen to grab a bottled water. My mother hadn't been around for four years now, but Vern had eyes on her without my dad knowing. My dad wrote her off when she refused rehab and chose drugs over us. My mother had a bad car accident, and that caused her to become addicted to pain killers, which then spiraled out of control and right to street drugs.

I came home one day to her laid out from an overdose and even then, after going to the hospital she walked out and went to get high. It was no hope I guess for her, so we all gave up trying. I used to go looking for her and cry myself to sleep over her now I don't even think about her anymore she isn't a mother so why should I want her.

"Where are you heading to, baby girl?" my father asked while counting out some money and placing it on the counter in from of me.

"I'm going to a party with Tori at her cousin's house in Baldwin Hills," I lied through my teeth, looking at my imaginary text messages avoiding eye contact. I knew if I told him the party was in Inglewood, he wouldn't let me go.

"Ok well, be safe and don't be out there drinking and doing drugs. Don't take no drinks from no guys at all. Rich black boys slip roofies in your shit," my dad replied while eyeing me suspiciously. My uncle called him to head out and thank God because now he was out my hair.

I was just about to call Tori when I heard a horn blow outside. I locked up and was out the door. I hopped in her car, and she was blasting "Back That Azz Up". I ain't even speak. I just smiled, slapped her five, and started dancing right along with her. We were having our own damn party in her car. We pulled up on the block, and the party was in full swing. We parked not too far and sat for a minute while Tori fixed her bob. Tori was a pretty chick and was hella thick and curvy. Tori pulled her purse from the back seat and went inside of it pulling out some small bottles of liquor. She passed me one, and we took them to the head. She told me she had a lot more in the bottom of her bag so we could drink our own shit and control our limit.

As soon as we stepped on the sidewalk, the guys started to make their passes at us and spit their corny lines. We kept it moving and headed into the house party. The music could be heard as we walked up and classic Uncle Luke blasted through the speakers. We made our way through the crowd and danced as we walked through the door. We found a spot by the back door that led to a backyard where people were outside doing the same thing as the people inside but also shooting craps. We decided to step outside as it was hot and sweaty and started to smell stale inside. Girls were all over the floor doing the crybaby and popping in slits just showing out. We stepped out in the backyard to a cloud of smoke.

I fanned it away from me and nudged Tori to pass me another shooter. I took it to the head feeling nice as we bopped to the music just taking in the scene. The craps game was intense. The guys laying was talking so much shit as they played at one point, I was convinced a brawl was sure to break out, but I guess my sheltered ass ain't know much of nothing because they laughed and slapped each other up after talking shit about each other's mommas. A crew of guys came walking into the backyard from the drive-way, and everyone was making their way to slap five and dap it up with the four guys. They all were decent looking, but the one that caught my attention and had me enticed by his presence was chocolate fine ass one.

I thought I was losing my mind when we made eye contact, and I looked behind me to see if he was possibly looking elsewhere, and that wasn't the case. He had his eyes on me, and the wink and kiss that he blew me confirmed that. I smiled and waved back before Tori pulled my ass to the side to talk. I was still stuck on him, so my eyes kept wandering to him as Tori talked and handed me another shooter. I hadn't heard a word she said because Mr. Chocolate had my ass lost in a trance. Tori noticed my attention wasn't there, and she followed my eyes to the man who had me stuck. We were engaged in a stare down, and my heart was skipping beats as he made his way over to us. Each step he took, I knew I would pass out any minute.

"Hello, beautiful, are you enjoying yourself?" the fine chocolate man asked.

I couldn't respond. I just shook my head like a damn mute as he smiled showing his perfect white teeth. None was missing, and there were no gaps in all thirty-two of his sparkly, white teeth. He had a low fade with waves and a nose ring in his nose. He gave me a bad boy vibe, but he spoke well like he was more than the bad boy persona. He stood next to me watching the craps game, and I was taken aback by his cologne. It smelled so good. I didn't know what brand it was, but it was my new favorite for a man. I knew most cologne from my dad and brother, but not this one. It was a plus in my book.

"The name is Kilondre, but everybody calls me Kilo," he stated, taking my hand and shaking it.

I was sweating, and my palms were moist. I wonder if he felt it. Shit, say something, Louve. You are messing up. I was having a long ass convo in my head and obviously too long because Tori interjected and saved my silly ass.

"Nice to meet you, Kilo. I'm Tori, and this is my homegirl Louve." Tori smiled and elbowed me, and I smiled back.

"It's nice to meet you beautiful ladies. My boy Drip is over there. I'ma bring him over." Kilo was about to go get his friend, but Tori stopped him.

"No need for that, I'm taking already," Tori replied proudly pulling her shirt down a little and pointing to Edge's name in the calligraphy writing. Tori was happy showing off my brother's name tattooed across her left breast. She quickly pulled her top back up covering most of the tat again.

"Oh, my bad miss lady, no problem. And what about you Miss Love?" he asked, taking my hand into his.

"It's Louve, and no I am not taken. I am newly single," I stated in a matter of fact tone.

"That's like music to my ears, sweetheart. Here take my number before I dip out." He took my phone from my hand, flipped it open, punched in his number, and then called it. He ignored the call and told me he would hit me up later. He kissed my hand and made his way out of the yard with his friends.

I smiled as I came from my thoughts of the past. Kilo and I had been through a lot, but our love was solid, and I was in love with him still to this day. Kilo was all I needed beside our kids, and we had a long road to go to get to the best part, but he was showing me that he was down for us. I knew in my heart that it was nothing that Kilo wouldn't do for us, and the way he went hard in the paint to provide and protect his family, made my heart swell. I didn't have that fancy rich shit you see on these shows or read in the books, but I had a man who was good to me and down for me ten toes to the concrete.

3

KILO

I never meant to snap on Louve like that and drop the bomb about Edge and me going back to the streets out of anger. I actually wanted to have a real conversation about it, not like this all mad and heated in the moment and midst of a blowout. Life was rough as hell right now, and I had to get it how I live the best way I knew how. My love for Louve was deep as hell, and that would never change. She and my kids meant the world to me, and it was time for me to give them the life they deserved, not this struggle shit we were going through now. The days of us having to live paycheck to paycheck were over. I had to get out here and get it off the muscle. The money was the motive to my madness right now, and unfortunately, I had to go back on my word of never going back to the streets. Edge wanted me to be the distro for all of Miami, while he remained the plug branching off to other cities and states, and I was ready to take that title and get this money up.

I never had a family, and the streets were all I knew since I was ten years old. My mama Kima was a hustler, but she got caught up behind some nigga and his wife, and they shipped her upstate. I never got the full story on what occurred, and she never wrote and refused my visits, so when she turned her back on me, I turned mine too and faced the streets on my own. I was nine when they shipped my mother upstate to New York, and my Aunt Myra took me in. Myra only took me in for the money she'd get from being my foster parent. I was moved into an already overcrowded home in Inglewood. Although Auntie Myra was blood, we were far from family. She hated kids and felt by ten years old you needed to find a way to make some money to care of yourself and to put some of it back in her pockets.

She never showed us shit that would help us in life down the road in a legitimate lifestyle, but she made sure she showed us how to take what we needed and wanted or be a broke bum in her words. At ten, I was jackin' niggas around the city hopping out at night from a bush and taking what I wanted. The stick-up kids, look out boys, nickel and dime hustlas, it didn't matter. I'd jack them all. Whenever I saw an opportunity, I took it. I didn't want that life, but I was forced into it, and I could never shake that adrenaline rush once it kicked in. Eventually, I moved on to a crew of hittas just like me. I linked up with my homie Drip when I was twelve. He was a cool ass dude who was a natural born hustler. We linked up through his cousin Muse. Muse was a money hungry nigga, and he got money any way possible.

Muse ran a crew of hittas that were responsible for different areas of the business. Muse had pay-for-hire hittas, heist hittas, drops and deliveries, gun suppliers, chop shop boys, and stick-up boys. Anything you needed, we offered at the right price. Muse linked Drip and me together for a few heists, and when we delivered with no mix-ups or issues, he put us on his team, and it's been on since then. The one area we hadn't tapped into was the drug business. Pushing weight was a big move, and me personally, I wasn't too interested in the problems that came from that. The jobs we did never get back to us because we covered our tracks.

In this drug shit, people watched you and always felt they could take your spot. There was always a nigga ready to attack and bitches doing setups. I wasn't pressed for none of that shit, so I never tried to hug the block. I stayed in my lane and did what I did on my terms, my way. Muse had other plans though, and he tasked me with finding him a supplier. I had done some work for this cat name Edge a few times, and he always tried to pull me on his team, but I was loyal to the soil. There weren't no switching sides over here. There was no beef, but that was how I did things. Loyalty and respect go a long way. Edge respected it, and fell back on that and kept business with us.

I had to meet up with Edge one day for a gun order, and since he only requested me anytime he did business, Muse used that to put his plan in place. I presented the deal to Edge and to my surprise, he was on board and even fronted us a few keys. Once we flipped those and made that money in no time, it was a go from there. Shit was rolling and rocking for a year before I met Louve. I saw her fine ass at a house party and knew that I had to have her. The fucked-up part was I had no clue that she was my plug's baby sister. Once word spread about us, Edge was on my ass and gave me hell the whole first year.

The tension started to put a strain on our business relationship, but when they father got locked up, Edge had no choice but to let me take care of Louve plus she was pregnant. Louve had no clue that Edge was who I was working for, and we kept it that way for good reason. Edge knew my team was official, and he ain't want to lose his hittas or that money for the work. Edge still kept trying his hand at getting me to join his team and leave the crew alone and focus on the big bags like he was bringing in, but I knew greed got you killed or locked up, and I was cool staying in my lane. I wasn't even feeling the streets, and Edge knew that. I did the pick-ups and drop-off exchanges, but I passed that over to Muse who gave it to the workers he had on the block.

I was content with the shit we were doing before the deal with Edge. I was considering putting Drip in my place because he loved that street shit. He was built for it. I wasn't letting Edge cause no issues with Louve and me. Now that she was in my hands, he had no say on anything with us. When they father got locked up and charged with thirty years, Louve came to stay with me in my little studio apartment. It wasn't a big ass house like they pops had before the FEDS seized it, and it wasn't a dope ass condo like Edge and Tori's spot, but it was ours. I let her come in and decorate it how she wanted since all I had was a bed and a TV. Louve had just graduated from high school and was pregnant with our firstborn, KJ.

Edge was pissed, but me, I was the happiest man alive, and Louve was excited too. I fell even deeper in love with her the day Louve gave birth. Things were good, and I was still out here making moves, bending corners, and rolling with the Hittas. Louve wasn't a fan of it, but she was a rider and down for her man. She fell in love with a real hitta, and it was no turning back now. Life moved fast, and before I knew it, we had three kids and were now renting a three-bedroom townhome. I had dreams of going legit, but money talked and bullshit walked, so I kept going with what was working for us. One day I would open my sneaker store and dispensary shop and flip a few houses, but for now, the streets were calling.

Shit started to get hectic when some niggas out east stepped out of line causing me and Drip to make an example out of them one night at a local basketball game. We were clearly mistaken at what the niggas would do afterwards. I was always ready to square up I didn't shoot niggas for fun or in a fight, I did that shit for money. The only time I used my gun was when it was my life or theirs or because I got paid to knock a nigga off. Otherwise, I was throwing them hands all day. Shoot me a fade any day. That gun shit wasn't to play with. Shit was rolling good until one day them niggas pulled up and sprayed up Drip's trap, catching me in my low rider off guard.

My life flashed before my eyes being shot three times. One shot was to the chest. It went through and through. It caused no major damage to arteries, but my lung was punctured, so I struggled with breathing for a while. One grazed my head causing a lot of blood loss, almost taking me out, and one was stuck in my hip still to this day. I thought I was a goner that night, but somehow God got me back here, and I was determined to leave the crazy shit that I was doing behind and doing right by my family. Louve was two months pregnant at that time with our fourth child, but all the stress and shit along with her not eating or taking care of herself caused her to have a miscarriage.

I laid in that hospital for three weeks before I was released home with all these meds, breathing treatments, and physical therapy. And after all that, Louve was there to help me. Even though she was looking defeated and like a bag of bones having lost a crazy amount of weight, she nursed my ass back to health and I, in turn, did the same for her. I got her to get back to herself, and she started picking that weight back up. They say good dick a do that to you, so that's what I did. I also wanted to reconnect after almost dying. She was all I wanted every day. Once I was back to damn near 100%, I went and got my forklift certification and started working at a warehouse. I became a regular Joe Shmoe with a nine to five and a family at home.

Now, here we are a year later, and I'm about to walk back into that life. The only difference is this time I was the connect, and I wasn't about to be on the block or in the trap. I weighed my odds and made my mind up way before I even let the shit slip out to Louve. I knew she was pissed, but she would soon see it was all gone be worth it. I wanted to give Louve all she deserved and then some. And now with another baby, I really had to get shit in order around here for my family.

I shot Edge a text and let him know it was out, and Louve knew about the shit we were in to. I didn't get a response, but he read it, and that's all I needed. Now I had to make shit right with my baby.

4

DRIP

I sat posted up in a chair against the front door blocking it and had my Pitbull Homie at the back door standing guard so that Egypt couldn't get out. I don't know why Egypt tried me every chance she got. She was trying to leave this house dressed like she wasn't a wholesome woman, with a nigga at that who was certified crazy, especially over her fine ass. My tactics were starting to get more and more extreme because she was using the power of her honey pot to cloud my mind. She had pounced on me like a damn lioness in heat when I came in the house a few hours ago. She was using her yoga moves and her pole lesson classes on me and had my nose wide open.

After getting it in, I dozed off into a good ass sleep until I heard her loud ass friends on speakerphone in the bathroom about going to some kickback in Baldwin Hills. I hopped up quick as hell and headed right downstairs to see what she was gone wear. I had just ripped up some little ass skirt and top to match that looked like a damn Band-Aid across my titties. Yes, my damn titties, that ass belongs to Dreon "Drip" Alves. I damn near was tempted to just tell her ass that she couldn't go period, but I was gone be cool and see what was up.

An hour went by before I got too damn impatient and went upstairs to see what her ass was doing. I pushed her dressing room door open, and for a minute, her beauty blinded me. She was dressed in a lace thong and push up bra. She stood in the mirror and applied her makeup. She wore her natural curls down and wild how I loved. Her body was glowing from whatever shimmer oil she had on, but my insanity kicked back into gear when she retrieved a dress from the chaise lounge. The dress had a hole cut in the back and the front and snapped around the neck. She wasn't going anywhere in that shit, and I meant that.

"Are you having fun trying on makeup and clothes not to go nowhere?" I asked, startling her.

"Dreon, you scared the shit out of me. I thought you were sleep," she replied, sliding the dress on ignoring what I asked her.

"So, you're still gone put the dress after what I just said. Hahaha play with me if you want to, E. You might as well take all that shit off. We are staying in the house tonight. It's Netflix and chill and all that, so come on bring your apple head ass on downstairs I'ma go pop the popcorn.

"Dreon, I'm going out, and I'll be home before midnight." She went into her shoe closet like shit was all good. I laughed and headed downstairs.

And here I am now stationed at the door waiting for her to try and get up out of here. I started playing Words with Friends killing these people with my vocabulary. I got an incoming call just as Egypt came down the stairs.

"What up Kila Kilo, what's good?" I asked watching Egypt like a hawk as she switched items out her big purse and into her little one.

"Nothing much brah, I'm about to head on out here handle some business with Edge. We need you on board tomorrow, playboy," he said talking in code.

"Oh, fo sho, you know I'm wit it, but let me hit you back. Egypt is over here testing my gangsta trying to take her big ass head out the house in half of nothing. Bro, she got life twisted!" I spat loudly so that Egypt could hear me.

"Mannn, leave that girl alone dawg. Let her live, shit. I wish she could take Louve's ass out with her. She's been stressing me out," he replied, laughing.

"Man fuck all that, I'm posted in a chair at the front door. I ain't playing with her ass. She ain't going out here dressed like she ain't a woman with a man at home. Hell naw," I said, snatching her keys off the hook.

"Bro, yo ass is certified crazy. I know they give you a check for that shit hahaha. Leave lil sis alone. She works hard, so let her live. But y'all be easy, I'ma hit you tomorrow," he stated, hanging up right after.

"Dreon, give me my keys so that I can go. I have the girls waiting on me," she whined, stomping her foot.

"They gone be waiting all night because you not coming, now go change for movie night," I replied, kissing her cheek and walking off to the kitchen.

I had all the keys in my pocket. I heard her stomp up the stairs and slam the door, so I took off to the bottom of the stairs and yelled up to her.

"You can stomp yo feet and be mad, but it's a waste of time. Come chill with your man and stop acting like a brat!" I yelled out.

She didn't open the door, but I could hear her going off and talking to her pack of hyenas about what I just did. I popped the popcorn, poured some drinks, and sat on the couch to watch some shows. I shot Egypt a text to come down, and she sent me back the middle finger. All I could do was laugh when she stomped her ass down the stairs and sat on the couch next to me. She tried to reach for the popcorn, but I moved it out the way.

"Give me some popcorn, Drip," she whined.

"Not until you give me a kiss," I said, puckering my lips out.

"Ugghh you get on my nerve with yo big head ass. You so damn petty, Dreon," she complained, but leaned over and kissed me on the lips and snatched the popcorn out my hand.

5

EDGE

I was ten seconds from knocking this broad Kelli out. The pretty girls had a tendency to get me, but they always ended up pissing me the hell off. I gave her ass a job at the reception desk of my car dealership on the strength that we had history. I slipped up and let her suck my dick, and now she's in here trying to create drama with Tori. That's a guaranteed way to get her ass fucked up. Tori was my heart, and even though I had a few years on her, we were connected and on the same level. I cheated here and there, but I was trying the last six months to get my shit together before she left me or killed my ass. Tori was a Pitbull in a skirt and played no games with my ass. We done had some crazy ass shit happen, and it was always when I was caught up doing her dirty. The last time, she locked my ass in the basement for a day and a half, and I was scared she was about to murder my ass. I had been on my best behavior before Kelli started working here.

Tori told my ass to hire her gay ass cousin to work the reception, and I refused, not because he was gay, but because the sexy ladies always helped bring in the buyers. However, I was now considering it since Kelli was currently hiding under my desk as I FaceTimed with Tori. I wouldn't have been worried if she wasn't close to being here.

Kelli's ass was steady trying to put my dick back in her mouth, and I was struggling because she was stroking my balls perfectly, and I damn near was ready to moan aloud. I kept pushing her off, but she wasn't letting up, and I know it's because she knows Tori is right on the phone. Kelli was a pass around looking to snag a big-ticket nigga to provide her the lifestyle she wanted.

Once the call dropped, I snatched my dick out of Kelli's mouth, and her extra ass made it make a pop sound like I took a lollipop out her mouth. I glared down at her shaking my head as she slowly crawled from under the desk. I didn't even look at her as she slid by me as I made my way to the bathroom. I had some important shit to handle tonight, and she wants to be in here causing extra stress unnecessarily.

Before she closed the door, I called out to her, "Yo, Kelli, take a week off and get your shit together. By the time you come back, I expect you to act professionally and accordingly."

I watched as she nodded her head on the verge of tears from my stern tone. She slammed the door shut, and I cleaned myself up. Tori hadn't called back, and I decided not to call her just in case she was on bullshit with me. I would wait it out and see where her head was since I didn't know if she heard something or not.

I checked the front and Kelli had been long gone but left the mail for me. I opened the envelope with the photos I had been waiting on. I called up my boys Fresh and Deck to bring this nigga Troy up to the shop. I had waited long enough and gave Troy ample amount of time to come to me with the shit to at least prove he was loyal to this team, but he failed to do so, and now the pictures proved what Drip told Kilo and me about this clown. Troy was working for the Mexican Cartel to set us up and take our territory from the Columbians that I worked with, but that was the least bit of our problems because Troy was an FBI informant and was trying to kill two birds with one stone and take us all down.

I was able to reach an acquaintance of The Dons of the Lopez Mexican Cartel and set up a meeting. Once I got all the info that I needed from Troy before I offed his ass I'd be on my way to Cozumel,

Mexico to meet with them, give them the info, and possibly create an
alliance, which would mean more money for us all. The beef that ran
between these two cartels Lopez and Esteban was decades long, but a
nigga like me saw an opportunity to end the shit and get money
together. They could either jumped on board and used our connects
at the FBI, or face them charges that were being worked on against
them. They really ain't have much choice, so I already put Mr.
Esteban up on game. He supplied me with the best pure cocaine the
U.S. ever saw, and in return, I made him boatloads of money without
him ever having to step a foot on U.S. soil.

I saw the trucks pull around back and I shut off all but the showroom lights off and made my way to the back after locking the doors.
Tonight, the side of me I tried to keep at bay was coming out to play,
and I was getting an adrenaline rush just thinking of the way I was
gone crack this niggas jaw for playing with me. I reached the back
just as they dragged a bound-up Troy from the trunk of the Navigator.
I opened the basement door, and we headed down to where I
handled my other business in a soundproof room. Once they tossed
him on the ground and pulled the pillowcase off his head, he started
to turn his head frantically seeing the menacing look I was giving
him. He couldn't speak with the duct tape over his mouth, but he
could see and hear me, and now he was gone feel me and my wrath.

6

LOUVE

I didn't talk to Kilo the whole ride home. Even though I knew I loved him, I was still mad at his outburst and the way he dropped that bomb on me, and he didn't even try to say anything to me. We scooped up our kids, and he took us home, but he left right back out. I didn't even bother with asking him where he was headed because truthfully, I was still pissed, and I'd probably just say some slick shit that will have us in here beefing and I ain't in the mood for that.

I got the kids bathed since they had already eaten dinner at Tori's place. Once the kids were situated, I warmed up my plate of food that Tori sent for us. I put Kilo's plate in the fridge and sat at the card table that we had set up as a dining room table. I was in heaven as tore down the meatloaf, mashed potatoes, gravy, and corn on the cob.

Tori could burn in the kitchen and cook just about anything. I learned many cooking tips from her. I read through the pile of mail as I finished up my food, and a letter had come from the contest Tori had entered my art into. I hadn't won first place, but I was runner up and was invited to attend an all-expenses-paid trip to New York for an art seminar and workshop. I was also given brochures on different programs and schools for art and career info. I dreamed of things like this, but my family came first. I would, however, consider my options. It was only a few week's long program, and I'd be back home with my family right after. I already knew Kilo would try to tell me no, but I think this was a decision that I was making with or without his support. I had done anything Kilo wanted, and I hoped he would do the same for me.

I was exhausted and decided to take a hot shower so that I could unwind. I stepped into the shower and felt like I was in heaven. The water cascaded over me, and it was the most relaxing feeling that I'd ever had. The Bluetooth shower speaker hanging on the wall of the shower played my favorite song currently "Girls Need Love" by Summer Walker. I could stay in this shower forever with the way it made me feel, but I'd start to shrivel up, so I got out after about twenty minutes. Once out, I dried off then rubbed my body down with cocoa butter. I threw on Kilo's baseball jersey as a nightshirt and climbed in our bed.

I shook my head at the sound of the air mattress as I flopped onto it. It was the nicest air mattress money could buy, and if Edge knew the shit we struggled with over here, I'm certain he would kick my ass for not coming to him. Kilo did what he could off the job he had, but multiple layoffs got us here. We started with a small apartment and then upgraded to a townhome, which I now realize was our problem. We were young and dumb and never saved or invested. After Kilo got shot and we had no money was coming in, I had to sell everything just to get us food and pay bills all because Kilo refused to let my brother help us.

Now, after the eviction from the townhouse, we were in a small ass apartment and barely making it here. I figured if Kilo were going back to the streets without talking it over with me, then he would have to deal with what I was about to do. I was going to get a loan from my brother and a job. I needed to do something for me, pregnant or not. I had so many thoughts running wild. They soon calmed down, my eyes got heavy, and I crashed right to sleep.

I WAS AWAKENED from my sleep by the pleasure my body was feeling and my own moans that I hadn't realized I was making. When my brain focused, I was hit with a wave of intense pleasure. I lifted my head to see Kilo going beast mode on my kitty. He had my legs pushed back and spread out limiting my movements. I unbuttoned the jersey I fell asleep in freeing my breasts and toying with my swollen nipples. I massaged my right breast with one hand letting the other run through Kilo's waves. With the tongue lashing that he gave my lips, and the way he was stroking my center with his tongue, my mind was gone. Kilo was apologizing with his tongue, and I was accepting it with open legs.

My orgasm tore through me causing me to grip his head tighter as I released a flood that he eagerly licked up. That orgasm was a high like no other. I couldn't even fully recover before Kilo had me face down in the air mattress and filling me up. The sloppy splashing of his dick as it slid in and out of me was turning me on even more than I was. The way he slowly stroked and hit my spot repeatedly had me biting the pillow moaning into it with a muffled voice. The feel of his balls as they slapped my clit sent a wave of pleasure throughout my body. I was nearing my climax and started to throw my ass back matching his thrust. All that could be heard throughout the room, besides our panting and moaning, was the slapping sounds of our skin, my ass as it hit into his pelvis, his balls as they slapped my clit, and the slaps he delivered to my ass as he stroked in and out.

"You still love me?" he spoke into my ear, licking along my neck. That caused me to shudder in ecstasy.

"Yesss, Kilo! I love you!" I moaned out as he slapped my ass, causing it to ripple. He gripped my cheeks in both hands spreading my ass apart using it as a guide as he stroked faster going deeper and hitting my spot head-on.

"Ohhh baby, right there! You're hitting my spot!" I cried out in pure satisfaction from the dope dick that he was giving me.

"I love you Louve, don't you ever forget that. Fuckkkk! This pussy is wet as hell!" he growled out loudly as he neared his peak. I was right there too on the verge of exploding.

"I'm cummming!" I yelled as we both climaxed.

I fell flat into the bed too spent to move a muscle. Kilo got up from the bed, causing me to sink into the air mattress a little. I could hear him running water in the bathroom, and then he was back wiping me down before climbing back into the bed with me.

"I'm sorry for snapping on you earlier, and I promise you I'm not out here living recklessly. This move I just made is major. We're gone be set. Just trust your man, ok?" he asked, waiting on my reply.

I rolled over to face him and stared at him before leaning in and kissing him passionately.

"I trust you, Kilo," I assured him as he ran his hand along my arm.

I laid my head on his chest and said a quick prayer for us, our family and especially for Kilo. I was down to ride for him through whatever, and it wasn't a doubt in my mind that he was all I wanted. All I needed in this life of sin was Kilo and our kids. We laid there talking about what he would be doing, and he told me to go house shopping first thing in the morning. We would no longer be living in the cramped apartment but moving into a house. He'd delivered as promised to Edge and received a nice little piece of change as a token of Edge's appreciation. Pretty soon we would be homeowners, and Kilo promised me a ring and a wedding finally.

I had my concerns and reservations about the work he would be doing, but I loved Kilo, and I trusted my man with my life and our kids, so if he said it's all good and he got us, then I was gone rock with it. I couldn't wait to find us a nice ass house and decorate it. We would have a home now to call our own with no more air mattresses or card tables. I didn't mention the trip just yet to New York, but I would once we got settled. For now, I wanted to enjoy this makeup session, and round two was about to go down. I slowly slid down as Kilo smoked on his blunt placing kisses along his ripped abs, and like always, that anaconda was brick and at attention and I wasted no time blessing my man with my warm mouth.

7

TORI

Once LouLou grabbed the kids, I straightened the house and was on my way to get my man. He worked too hard, and I wanted him to myself tonight. I was headed there this morning but got caught up with LouLou and Kilo. So, when our FaceTime call got disconnected, I didn't even bother him since he seemed busy anyway. However, it was damn near midnight, and I hadn't heard from him, so I decided I should pull up on him. I wasn't insecure in the least bit, but Edge was known to have hoes before he settled down, and sometimes players relapse. I was understanding of the temptations, but when I pull the same shit, he gone lose it, and I tried to stress that to him without actually doing it. However, I warned him. One more fuck up and he was gone feel exactly how I felt, and then he would understand.

He tried to hide the last bitch that I caught him with in his basement. This was before I moved in and we really made shit 100% exclusive, but still, he had just flipped out over a nigga paying for my gas at the store. So if we were on, then cool cut your hoes loose and tie up loose ends, and we Gucci all the way around.

Well apparently, he missed that memo, and I popped up with the key he gave to me. I arrived back home early from a business trip a day early, and low and behold he was living the bachelor life. I parked right in his driveway and made my way catching him on his way to the basement, in his boxers with some whipped cream and fruit on a platter. He looked like a deer caught in headlights seeing me standing there.

I didn't even speak. I charged right to the door, but he had slammed closed and blocked it. I kept pushing him to get down there, but to his surprise, his untrained side hoe made her up and pushed the door opened that he pushed back closed again. We all stood there for about ten minutes with him blocking her in, me pulling his heavy ass, and her trying to push the door open. I finally lost it and slapped the shit out of him, causing him to charge at me. We were entangled with me hemmed up and clawing at him when his fucking neighbor came busting her way out from the basement in nothing but a thong and some heels. I lost all sense I had and started fucking his ass up the minute he let me down and tried to hurry her out.

This bitch done had us over with her man for barbecues and these idiots in here fucking like long lost lovers. I was livid and ready to body his ass. He ran to the basement to retrieve her stuff while she tried to play cat and mouse as I chased her around. Well, I had news for them. She wasn't leaving this house with shit. I slammed the basement door and locked it with the bolts and all. She watched on in fear, and the minute I was done with the last bolt, I charged for her, but she made her way out the front door and ran across to her home making it inside before I could reach her.

I had just got to her door when she slammed it shut, but luck was on my side when her man pulled up in his work truck. I stopped beating on her door and went to tell him about his whore of a girl. I told him everything, and I could see the anger in his eyes as he listened to me spill all the tea. I told him if he didn't believe me ask her where her phone and stuff is at and why I was beating on the door. I left him standing there to contemplate as I went back inside Edge's home. He was banging on the door to get out, but fuck that. I wasn't about to let his ass out. I left with the platter of fruit, and I left his dirty ass to rot down there. At least he had a half bath down there but no way out thanks to him making it a secured room for his business meetings and parties. Almost two days went by before I finally let Louve go and let him out the basement after she started to panic about him missing. Once I let her inside the house, I was out. I took the first thing smoking miles away, and I ghosted his ass for a week before he found me and now here we are.

I'm for certain that he is smarter than that now. I think that day and a half in the basement gave him a new frame of mind on how to not fuck with me. I was cool and chilled for the most part, but I had that evil side in me, and Edge knew that. So, as I made my way to him now, I knew we were good, and he wasn't out here playing me. He was probably tied up with the dealership or with his many other business ventures. Either way, I knew he knew better than to be fucking with a bitch.

I pulled into the parking lot of Buyer's Edge Luxury Cars Dealership. I checked myself out, and I was looking good even with a bare face. My edges were laid, and my hair was pulled up in a neat top knot on my head just the way my man liked it. I applied a little lip gloss and grabbed my keys out the ignition.

I strutted my way to the door and attempted to pull it open, but it was locked. The lights in the showroom were on, but the rest of the place was dark. I called up Edge, and it rang a few times before I got his voicemail. I decided to go around back where Edge's reserved spot was and where his office window was located. As I neared the corner, I could hear some commotion, and as soon as I rounded that brick wall, I was frozen in place as I watched Edge smoking a blunt as his two men held a guy upside down. The guy looked badly beaten, and I was about to turn around but wasn't fast enough to not witness Edge pull out his gun and send one bullet right between the guy's eyes. I gasped and stumbled back and obviously bought attention to me. I had never seen a person's head blown open like that, and I felt my Caesar salad about to rise.

I knew the man Edge was, but I hadn't seen for myself how ruthless he could actually get in a very long time and even then, it was only him beating someone, but never anything like this. I locked eyes with Edge who placed his gun back behind his back in the band of his pants. He gave them orders I guess to get rid of the guy, and I just watched as they began to wrap his body in bubble wrap and then tarp. I hadn't even realized the tears were falling until Edge was on me wiping them away. He didn't even explain himself at all to me, and I should have asked. I should have made him give me an explanation, but did I really want to know the reason. I allowed him to kiss me passionately and then lead me in the back door of the building leading to his office and back storage room.

We entered the office with still no words spoken, and he locked the door behind us. I had so many thoughts running through my head, but I couldn't bring myself to speak them aloud. I watched as Edge just puffed away on his blunt. He motioned for me to come over to him by his desk. He pulled my leggings down, and my thong soon followed. He laid me on top of his desk spreading my legs wide. I watched as he traced a finger from my navel down to my honey pot. He traced along my lips and folds teasing me. His hands were strong, but his touch was soft and soothing to me. When he dipped a finger inside me and slowly stroked me, making the splashing sounds that he loved when he played in my wetness, all thoughts of the dangerous man he is left my mind.

I only had thoughts of feeling him inside me taking my body on a high that only he could give me. Edge was dangerous but never towards me. My heart was his, and he knew that shit too, which is why he had me on this desk about to have his way with me and fuck the fear I may have had out of me. This isn't the first time I saw the side of him. It's been a while, but I saw him beat a nigga to death with a brick and his bare hands for disrespecting me. As my thoughts ran wild, I was jolted back to reality when Edge slid in me slowly. I looked him in his eyes as he slowly stroked in and out of me. I loved this man beyond words and to a capacity that scared me, yet enticed me. I always wanted more. I needed more of him, and that was what I got.

Edge was working me, and now he had me pulled down to the end of the desk with my legs pushed back almost to my ears. He used my legs as his support as he gave me deep strokes so that I could feel every inch of him. Edge wasn't lacking in the length or girth. He reached spots and made me feel things that I had never experienced before. I always thought squirting was a myth, but the way he was deep thrusting in and out of my sloppily wet center, I knew what was coming. I felt the muscles in honey pot tighten causing him to bite his bottom lip and close his eyes. We were both near that mark. After a few more strokes, I was squirting and cumming like a broken faucet, and Edge followed suit never pulling out, and my dick silly ass just laid there satisfied, not worried that he was trying to plant a seed.

"I love you, Tori," Edge spoke softly into my ear as he laid on me with his semi-hard dick still inside me.

"I love you too baby. You're not slick either," I replied as I laughed at him trying to hurry up and go inside his office bathroom.

"What are you talking about, girl?" he yelled from the bathroom over the water that he now had running in the sink.

"You ain't use a condom, and you didn't pull out. Edge, stop trying to get me pregnant before you even put a ring on my finger. Plus, I have one semester left, and I plan to start my interior design business right after graduation. Baby, we talked about this," I stressed while gathering my things and going into the bathroom with him.

"I can't help it, Tori. You got some good ass pussy. I can't just stop and pull out. I be in the moment, and you know damn well I'ma marry you. Shit, I said let's go to Vegas, baby. I'ma be thirty-five next month. I'm ready. You're the one playing with me," he replied, trying to act all hurt.

I didn't even press the issue any further. I just laughed his ass off and handled my hygiene so that we could go home. Any other bitch would have run far away from a man like this, but not me. I was head over heels for Edge, and I'd ride through whatever with him and for him. We had a crazy kind of love, but it was ours, and it was all I needed.

8

EGYPT

I had reached the point in my relationship with Drip that I no longer trusted his word, and that angered me because I never thought we would get to that point. At the beginning of our relationship, not a soul could tell me he was out here doing me dirty, but now five years later, I was for certain he was out doing all the things he said he never would do. When he started to change the way he handled me and started to do things out of his norm, I tried to tell myself not to trip and just wait it out, but tonight he confirmed he was now lying to me about his whereabouts. I called him after I left work, which my hours are normally eight to four, but I wanted to branch out into styling fashions for clients and coordinating events, so my boss gave me the opportunity tonight.

There was a video that a top rapper was shooting in a hotel in downtown Miami, so I was sent to style the girls and the rapper as well as make sure props, and different decorations were in place. I was one of the last ones to leave the shoot at around eleven at night after declining multiple invites to hang out, especially from Pras, the assistant director of the video. He was an up and coming director who was making a name for himself and constantly tried to shoot his shot at me in passing at my job. I worked for an image and PR consulting firm, and we had other areas that we offered expert services and styling our clients was one.

When I got promoted to lead image consultant, after a lot of backlash from other the only other black girl Koi, specifically my arch rival at Miami Image, Pras took immediate notice once I was put on their account. His advances were a waste because I had Drip, and he was all the man I wanted and needed. After all the crew and models left, I finally headed home.

As I left the hotel garage, I spotted a car that I knew all too well. I pulled up right along the rear of Drip's car and dialed him up. The phone rang and almost rolled to voicemail until he finally picked up. I asked him where he was for two reasons. One, I was hoping he'd meet me for some late night eats, and two, to see why he was here. I knew what Drip did for a living, so I was expecting him to say he had a meeting or something, but for him to flat out lie to me hurt. He told me he was at the trap and wouldn't make it home until more than likely after four a.m.

Now it's not even the first of the month, so all the red flags started to go off, but I played it cool and told him I'd see him in the morning. I went to get me some food and a bottle of Patrón, and I brought my ass right back to that hotel. I found a parking spot in the front lot of the Sheraton instead of the dark garage across the street. Although there were two other hotels in walking distance, I knew to park in the ramp or garage. You had to have a room and a door key to get in and out from the Sheraton since it was their garage. I sat for hours watching as people left in and out to return from a night out or start their night. I was just about ready to call it a night around 4:15 until I heard Drip's laugh.

My heart dropped into the pit of my stomach as I watched him laugh and flirt with Koi, my arch nemesis, in front of the hotel. Apparently, they were waiting on valet to bring their cars to them. With tears threatening to fall from the brim of my eyes I blinked them back, and I jumped out the car and stormed right over to them. They were so wrapped up in the conversation that they were having that they never saw me coming like a bat out of hell. I was so mad and hurt all in one, and I let that out right on Dreon.

"Is this the type of shit we on now, Dreon?" I yelled, causing them both to look like deer caught in headlights.

"Baby, what's up what are you doing here?" Drip asked, stepping to me and blocking Koi.

"Nigga, I want to know what the fuck you doing up here? This doesn't look like the trap to me! Well, my bad because that bitch is a thirst trap, thirsty ass hoe!" I screamed, causing some by passers to stop and be nosey. I didn't care the show was just beginning too.

"Egypt, calm down, it ain't what you think. I was coming from dealing with a business associate and bumped into her," he pleaded to me holding my hands as they shook with so much anger. I probably would have believed his story had Koi not blew up his lie.

"Oh, hell nah, Drip! You got me fucked up hahaha. Nah, lil miss perfect Egypt you got my job I should have had, but I had your man every weekend for the last three weeks, boo boo. He was loving the feel from the grip my fat cat had on his big ass dick riding that shit while you got lied to through the phone," she replied with so much hate in her voice.

I was ready to go at her ass too, but Drip snatched me up quick, and valet came right on time for her scary ass to scurry to her whack ass little '04 Honda.

"Get the fuck off me, Dreon!" I yelled, breaking from Drips embrace.

I glared at him, and the stupid ass look of guilt on his face and all I could do was turn and walk to my car before I ended up in jail. He fucked up for the last time. The little girls in the beginning that would play on my phone and all the immature shit we went through was supposed to be behind us. It's been five years, and we back at square one. I hopped in my car and sped home.

I tried to beat his ass to the house, but he was right on my ass. As soon as I was on the first stair of the porch, his ass had made it up in the driveway parking all crazy. I was so worked up that I couldn't get the key in the door fast enough before he was on the porch with me.

He started the same song and dance with the begging and pleading, and the endless promises to never do it again. I was sick and tired of hearing that shit. I was starting to feel a little buzzed, so I made my way to the room locking the door behind me.

Drip was on the phone going off on Koi for blowing his phone up, I assumed. That gave me the chance to make sure he didn't get in the room. I stripped out of my clothes showered and checked my phone. I had a $500 Cash App payment notification. When I opened it, it was listed as a *Tip from Pras*. At another point in time, I would have probably entertained him. Wait, I was getting Drip's cheating ass out my house in the morning, so maybe I will entertain Pras and take him up on that date request he shot out at me last week to talk business. I shot him a thank you text for the tip and climbed in the bed. I ignored Drip's knocks at the door and let the tears fall. Our relationship was on the brink of ending for good, and my heart was hurting.

THE NEXT MORNING, I woke up to the smell of breakfast. What many people didn't know was that Drip could cook— well mostly breakfast, fried chicken and grilling some barbecue. I dreaded getting up because I had to put my foot down. I loved Dreon, I truly did, but I couldn't let him think that he could keep doing this shit, and I'd just forgive him because I loved him. Nope, I loved me more, and I was gone get my respect, and if this didn't make his ass wake up and get it together, well then he can forget it forever.

I washed my face and brushed teeth, pulling my messy bedhead curls up into a bun.

I was all business when I started pulling all Dreon's shit out and pack into his luggage and duffle bags. I left the room after I filled them all up all of them to start on his shoe collection, which would require garbage bags. I walked into the kitchen, and my body almost betrayed me because that body built like a Greek god was on display as Drip cooked breakfast in only his boxers. When he smiled and winked at me, I swear I heard my kitty purr and drool. I squeezed my legs tightly together quickly to stop the pulsating that had begun and smashing my lips together from having my mouth hanging open in lust. I hurried by to the pantry and grabbed the box of trash bags.

I turned around to Drip right in my face holding a bouquet of red roses. I pushed past him and headed to the room, and he was hot my trail following me to the room. As soon as I entered the room, I started throwing bags into the hall, which caused his dog Homie to come barking acting a fool. I got so pissed about the shit with Koi all over again that I started packing the dogs shit too. I started dragging bags to the porch as Drip rambled on and on about being sorry. I lost my cool when he tried to once again downplay his cheating to a mistake that won't happen again, but the shit happened three times. That ain't no mistake. The nigga enjoyed that shit.

"You know what Drip, FUCK YOU! I've been riding and rolling for five years with your selfish ass, and you flip out if a nigga stares at me too long, but you're repeatedly fucking the bitch at my job who don't fucking like me. Nah, fuck this shit I'm about to do me my turn to have some fun around this motherfucker!" I yelled, storming past him back to the room to pack his sneakers.

"Yo Egypt, chill ma! Calm down and let's talk this shit I over. I didn't know Koi worked at your job, ma. I swear to God. I met her at the Gentleman's Palace, she came on strong as hell to me, and now I know why. I was stupid at as hell for that shot, and it will never happen again. I didn't mean to get caught up with that hoe. She did a little private dance for the fellas and focused in on me, and my dumb ass fucked up. I'm sorry, Egypt. I love you, shawty," Drip replied with a voice full of fear.

He should fear what happens because he fucked up, and I was taking a time out from him and his bullshit.

I didn't respond to him. I just went right back to packing his shit up and tossing it in the hall and down the stairs a little closer to the door and less carrying for me. He kept on talking, and I remained quiet until he tried to flip shit around. He began talking about the fact that I was working all the time, never home, and maybe if I had been at home more, then maybe his attention wouldn't have been so easily broken. I had to count to ten to keep from killing his ass. He had some nerve to try to blame me for his fuck up because he was too weak of a man to control his urges. I was working and holding us down the same way I did when he was just a runner and worker with the Hittas.

I just laughed at his ass directly in his face and kept on tossing his shit out. I was now just tossing sneakers out the front door at this point because he had pissed smooth the fuck off— no more miss nice Egypt. I was in straight bitch mode.

After all his shit from upstairs was outside or on the porch, I headed to his game systems and started unhooking that shit sitting it outside too. I then packed up all of Homie's shit including him. I placed Homie on the porch inside his cage. As I went back inside, Drip was coming from the kitchen fully dressed and carrying a box of what I had no clue. However, I overheard him on the phone telling someone to come get him because I was tripping.

I assumed it was Kilo or Muse since they were the only ones who knew where I lived. I had taken the car keys to the car he had parked all crazy in the driveway because that was one of my cars. His was in the shop. I went into the kitchen and hysterically laughed when I realized what he placed in the box. His petty ass took all the seasonings and meat out the kitchen that he brought. I didn't even give a fuck anymore as long as he left and gave me my space. I loved Drip, and he knew that shit, and that's why he did the shit he did because he knew I loved him and held him down all this time, but he was getting a rude ass awakening today because that girl I was is no longer residing here. I was gone get the love and respect I deserved, and if he couldn't give it to me, the next nigga will.

9

KILO

I had been up and out the house making moves but today was the day that I would be moving my family to our new home. I had finally got us out the small ass apartment, and that made me feel good that I was able to give my family a home of our own. Things with Louve and I had been going well, but I knew she wasn't feeling the early days and long nights. Louve was now eight weeks pregnant, and I had been thinking hard about proposing and once we were settled in our new home and things were all in line, I was gone give her a ring that she deserved.

I had to do some drops for Edge this morning, and the money I was pulling in just from a month of being his distro was the come up that I needed. My phone started to ring, and it was Drip calling.

"What up playboy, what you got going on for today?" I asked talking through my car's Bluetooth. Edge had gifted Louve and me with a whip each. She got a Land Rover to fit the kids in, and I got a new black on black Benz.

"Yo Kilo, come scoop me before I knock this goofy ass broad out man!" Drip roared into the phone.

"Say no more I'm pulling up on you in ten," I replied and disconnected the call making a sharp right onto the freeway.

I got to Drip in about twenty minutes, and when I pulled up, he was sitting on the porch with his dog and a bunch of bags and shoe boxes. I just laughed and shook my head because I knew Egypt must have put his ass out. I hopped out and walked up on the porch. Drip was looking stressed out, and shit so was his dog Homie. I had never seen a dog look so depressed before.

"Bro, what the hell is going on?" I asked, picking up a bag and following him to my trunk. I pooped the trunk, and we started loading the car up with all his things.

"Man, this damn girl tripping but I'm a tell you in the car I just want to hurry up leave before she gets back," he said, looking down the street like he was scared. All I could do was laugh at this crazy shit.

We got everything and the dog loaded in my car, and we were on our way to his hideout spot out in Baldwin Hills. Drip was quiet as he sparked up the blunt and passed it to me. I took some pulls off it and passed it back. He finally spoke up, and I just listened.

"I fucked up, Kilo. I was doing good too because I know Egypt is tired of my shit, but I done messed around and fucked her enemy at work. I had no clue they even worked together let alone couldn't stand each other. Actually, the bitch Koi is a hater ass bitch and mad that Egypt got the branch manager job over her, so she be filing internal complaints and shit trying to sabotage Egypt. Now, I'm thinking she set my ass up, and I fell for her trap," he stated, sounding defeated and tired.

"Just give sis a few days to cool off and y'all will be back like always," I said, trying to sound hopeful for my partna, but shit, I wasn't too sure either since last time was supposed to be the last time.

"Mannnn, I wish, but she is tripping on my ass. She done put me out and changed the locks, talking about she's about to live her best life. If Egypt starts talking to some clown ass nigga, I might lose my mind, Kilo. I love that damn girl, and she knows that I just be fucking up sometimes for no reason, but that doesn't mean I don't love her. She was on the phone with her crew dogging my ass out loud enough for me to hear from the outside. They are going out tomorrow, and

I'ma be there at Club 24K too, making sure she ain't with no niggas," he spoke through gritted teeth with his fists balled up.

I didn't even know what to say, so I just let him vent and get that shit off his chest. We ain't have no real business to tend to tomorrow. Surprisingly for a Friday, it was gone be a chill day. Edge was leaving out of town on business, so I decided to take my family out during the day to shop for our new home and babysit my homeboy at night to make sure he stays out of trouble. Shit was different now, and we had shit to lose. I was around for the turn-up but not no bull shit, so I'd be watching Drip to make sure that he was on point.

Drip gave me the full rundown of how Egypt caught him coming out of the hotel with this freak Koi he had told me about. He met Koi one night at the strip club, and they started fucking around, and now he gets caught with her ass by Egypt. He told me about them working together and being enemies. Females were just as trifling as he was. This broad Koi knew exactly who Drip was and who his girl was when she approached him, and she set his ass up good. Drip was looking sick behind this shit, and from the way, it sounds Egypt was really done playing games with his ass. I don't judge my niggas because I was young and dumb before too, fucking anything moving, but once I realized how good of a woman Louve was and how much I loved her, that shit was a no brainer to let go and settle down. I wasn't gone ever put myself in this type of shit that Drip was going through. The saying is never to say never, but I was confident in my ability to control my dick.

10

LOUVE

I was in heaven as I shopped at all the stores that Tori told me about. I was on FaceTime with Sherai who we hadn't seen or heard from in months since she moved to Atlanta, but my girl was moving back in a few weeks, and I couldn't wait. She was a married woman now, and I was so happy for her and Chase. Kilo just walked with the kids behind me as I talked and shopped away. He spared no expense, and I loved the fact that I was able to actually spend money and not wonder if it was our last. I finished up my call with Sherai and made plans to have dinner and do some double dating with the guys.

After hours of shopping, I had everything for the house that we needed from furniture all the way down to toiletries and groceries. The kids loved the new four-bedroom, four and a half bathroom house. KJ finally had his own room, and the girls got to share a beautiful Disney princess themed room. We had a formal dining room, family room, living room, a finished basement with a movie theater, and a huge eat-in kitchen. The master suite was something out of an *HGTV Extreme Homes* episode. We had a large picture window and a huge walk-in closet with shelves and hanger space for both of us on each side. The bathroom had the perfect spa tub and a waterfall walk-in shower. This house was a dream come true for my family. We finally had our own home.

As the movers unpacked us and got the furniture set up, I decided to do the kitchen so that I could cook dinner for my family our first night in our home. I got all the dishes washed and put in the cabinets and set the kitchen table with the decorative pieces I'd purchased for it. I cooked dinner and did laundry. We all sat the table as a family and ate dinner for the first time in a very long time. My family was making progress in a good direction, and I just prayed things stayed on the up and up. However, in the pit of my stomach, I knew that things were probably going to get rocky. That just seems to be the story of our life. I prayed it was just the jitters of happiness with this new move.

After dinner was finished, I got right to finishing the house. I don't know how, but I finished everything in the house and cleared out all the trash and boxes. I was in love with my dressing room. Kilo had a custom vanity made for me as well as a beautiful painting of me. The inspiration came from a picture in his phone that he'd snapped of me in a robe doing my makeup on one of our date nights from back in the day. Kilo made sure he had his man cave and gym in the basement, and the attic was converted into a theater and playroom for the kids. We had a huge indoor pool and Jacuzzi and an outdoor in-ground pool. This house was really our dream home. Kilo had the mind for real estate, so he researched and came upon a foreclosure, and instead of flipping it for money, he had it renovated for us. I couldn't wait to interior decorate the next house he decided to flip.

I got the kids ready and, in the bed, and then myself. Kilo had to head out, so it was just me in our huge king-sized bed watching reruns of *Martin*. I called up Tori, but got no answer and decided to call it a night. I then remembered all the important mail that was on my dresser, so I grabbed that and started to skim through it. There was a letter from my daddy, and I got so excited because I haven't heard from him in a while. Edge was still avoiding me, so I had no idea what our dad had been up to in there. I hated that my dad was locked up, but he felt since he did the crime, he would do the time, even if he was set up. He was facing twenty years, and I prayed the lawyer Edge hired could get him off or lower his sentence.

By the time I finished the letter, I was a mess crying and trying to figure out if I should do what my father asked. I never disobeyed my father, but this was a hard one to consider. My father asked that I find my mother and do what he was unable to do, which was help her get clean. My uncle had visited my dad in jail and told him my mother had gotten worse. He also told him it was time to stop acting like she wasn't out there hurting and in danger of dying any day from this shit. I was so mad at my mother when I was younger that I wrote her off and never attempted to go help her. I loved her, and she was once my idol, and the most beautiful woman ever, so I was hurt and confused when she chose drugs and running the streets over us.

To have my mother around and here to be a grandmother would be everything to me. A part of me wanted to find her and fix her up, but the other part was scared she would leave me again. This letter just placed a big load on me and right now, I didn't know if I had it in me to follow through with what my father requested. Time wasn't waiting, and I was scared that I would wait too late and she'd be dead, so in my heart, I knew what I needed to do. I guess I needed to sleep on this and then decide.

11

DRIP

I loved Egypt's bipolar ass. She was all a nigga needed, but shit, for some reason, she wasn't all I wanted sexually. I had bitches on me 24/7, and shit, sometimes I just wanted to have a little fun. It was just sex, nothing more than a physical attraction. There was no love for these hoes. She knew that, but this time, she might really be done giving my ass chances. I met Egypt when we were youngins in high school. She always had her shit together, and I admired her from afar. I was in and out of school doing the bare minimum just to get a diploma, but I noticed her even when she didn't notice me. I started taking an interest in football, and I was damn good too.

She was a cheerleader, so we started to see each other a lot during sophomore year. She had this whack ass boyfriend, some older cat she was fooling with thought he was Mr. Tough Guy called himself leaving her after she went off on him for being disrespectful. That was perfect for me because I swooped on in, walked her to the bus stop, and rode home with her. That became our routine. We would grab food, listen to music, talk about the fucked-up world we lived in, and just bond. Our connection was deep and solid, and I knew I had fallen in love for the first and only time. It was a wrap for anybody once Egypt got my heart and locked me down.

That friendship progressed into a relationship, and once I broke her virginity, it was a sealed deal. She was mine for life. Egypt loved my ass when I ain't have shit, and that's rare as hell because hoes want a nigga that got a nice ass car, his own crib, money to blow on them, and a big dick. I had the big dick and a sense of humor when we met, and she loved me still. I never meant to hurt her the way that I had, and the way I'm feeling now, I know that she had felt ten times worse. I was literally sick behind this shit. I didn't want to do shit but drink and smoke. I had been ignoring all calls and text because if it wasn't Egypt, then it wasn't shit for me to say. I started following her pages on all her social media accounts under a fake page just to see what she was up to. I had it bad, and I was letting the crazy side of me take over.

I was over here hurt than a motherfucker, and she was out living her best life. Today though, I was pulling up on her because I missed her like crazy, and we needed to talk. I ain't never have to go this long without her, and I was beating my own ass for the shit I did to her. I was reflecting on all the shit I had been doing, and I was doing some foul shit to a good girl. Egypt wasn't perfect, but she was perfect for me and didn't deserve the bullshit I had done to her. I had a real one who held her own and carried her weight, and here I was losing my queen for a bitch that I didn't care anything about. I was about to log out until I saw some nigga comment about how good she was looking last night, and he can't wait to take her out again.

My blood began to boil, and my eyes started to burn with fury. There was no way she was entertaining the next nigga, nah not my Egypt. I jumped my ass up quick, threw on some sweats and a tee, and was out the door. My once perfect beard was a mess as I took a glimpse of myself in my rearview mirror as I sat in my car contemplating calling her or just pulling up. The anger in me said fuck it and just pull up. I ain't showered or shaved in two days and I'm sure I smelled of alcohol, but I didn't care. I had to get my baby back, and that was now not later. I did ninety all the way to Egypt's townhome that we once shared. I didn't see her car, so I parked up a few houses and decided to wait on her.

Time dragged on as I dozed in and out of sleep while I waited. Sleep won the battle, and I was out until I had awakened to an almost dark sky and streetlights on as I sat up and adjusted my seat back upright. It took me a minute to remember where I was and why I was here. Then it dawned on me that I was supposed to be waiting on Egypt to get home, not falling asleep. I checked the time, and it was almost 7:30 at night and the street was quiet but full of cars. I started my car up and pulled out so that I could park in Egypt's driveway, but as I was nearing her house, I witnessed her coming out dressed in a sexy outfit with her curls piled on top of her head in a messy bun just the way I loved it. The skinny high waist jeans that she wore fit her like a glove and the pink low-cut V-neck crop top put her perfect caramel double D's on display. She wore her high heels with her pedicured pretty toes out and carried a pink hand-held purse. I was in awe as I watched her wave and smile as she came down her stairs.

I followed her gaze to the black BMW in her driveway with a license plate that read PRAS. The windows were tinted, so I couldn't see who it was, but I was growing more and more angry with each step she took. I tried to talk myself off that ledge of rage that I was on. Maybe it's one of her girls, and they are going out to do their own thing. She wouldn't have a nigga come pick her up. That's too intimate, nah not my Egypt, but I was wrong. I was wrong as hell, and the rage I felt right as I saw a tall, dark skin nigga step out the car and meet her at the walkway and lead her to the passenger side door was damn near uncontrollable. He opened the door for her, and I almost lost it as he bit his lip and grabbed the crotch of his pants, eyeing her round butt as she got in his car.

I waited as they pulled out the driveway, and then I proceeded to follow close behind them not losing them but not too close to bring attention to myself. It dawned on me that it was the same nigga from social media on all her pictures. I stayed a few cars behind and followed for twenty minutes until they pulled into the valet section of the Grand Amor restaurant. This place was known to be hella expensive, and on Fridays, there was live entertainment of some sort as they served a happy hour style menu and drinks. He held onto Egypt's lower back as they headed into the restaurant. I was beyond pissed off, and I wasn't letting her leave this restaurant with him. I waited, and about an hour and a half later they came out. They didn't head for valet though they walked across the street towards a bar.

I jogged to catch up, and just before they made it the front door, I pulled Egypt's hand from his. Egypt jumped, and he turned around in confusion looking between us as we just stared at each other. I took the opportunity to break the silence.

"You know me Egypt, and you know how I can get down. This is Dreon talking right now, but it's taking everything for me to keep Drip at bay seeing you with this nigga. I'ma ask you to dismiss him so that we can go work this out. It's no other choice, and if you want to spare him from what I'm capable of, I suggest you tell him now that this shit is a dub. Whatever y'all was doing or intended to do is over and done with," I stepped right in her space and spoke into her ear.

I saw her close her eyes and shudder at the sound of my voice and the feel of me close to her. She was missing the kid.

"Why are you doing this, Drip? You played around so much with me from day one, and I told you I wasn't dealing with your bullshit anymore. You can't just do as you please and play with my heart. I love you Drip, honest to God I do, but I refuse to be walked all over. You promised me you were done with the hoes and all that shit."

Her voice trembled, and the tears were sitting on the brim of her eyelashes ready to fall. She loved me still, but she was hurting, and I was ready to make shit right. I pulled her away from him so that we could have some privacy.

"Egypt, baby, I know I fucked up, and I'ma nigga who ain't have shit growing up. I had to get out here and get it out the mud, I made mistakes in life, but I learned and corrected them, and that's what I'm doing now with us. You are my rib. I've been sick without you, ma. Look at me. I look like shit because nothing mattered to me anymore. I made a terrible ass mistake because I was weak, and I will spend the rest of my life making it up to you. If you walk away right now, I'll let you go but I'm a kill that nigga over there just out of anger I'm not in my right mind, and I need you" I replied giving her a serious stare down as I spoke from the heart. I was a crazy ass nigga for sure, but I was crazy over her, and I didn't give a damn about anything but her right now.

No more words were needed after that. Egypt got that clown Pras to go on his way, and we headed to my hideout spot for the night. I decided we needed a weekend away from everyone and just spend some time alone to reconnect. We could go to the museum or some other corny poindexter shit she wanted. I wouldn't give a fuck as long as I with her. When we made it home, we talked about the things that needed to change, and Egypt had a nigga ready to shed a tear hearing her say she missed me too and loved me. We talked for hours before we showered together and got in bed.

I made love to Egypt that night something that I usually didn't do. We fucked all the time that porn star X-videos type of sex, but tonight was different. Tonight was necessary and reconnected us the way we needed.

I placed my hands behind my head as I watched Egypt ride me sexily. She had her eyes closed and held on firmly to each breast as she bounced up and down. I wasn't gone last long since this the first time in weeks I was getting any type of action. I closed my eyes and let her do her thing. My eyes shot open when she climbed off me, but a smile crept on my face as I saw her round ass was now facing me, and she slid down reverse cowgirl on my pole. I hope she knew what she just signed up for because I was about to tear her up, and I wasn't pulling out tonight. I was shooting her club up. My pull-out game was strong as fuck, especially with these birds, but with Egypt, my pull-out game was weaker than loose rubber bands.

12

KILO

I had to step in for Drip with the traps because he was locked up in the house making up with Egypt. I was worried about his ass for a minute. I didn't think Egypt would take his ass back. I hope my boy get his act together before he loses her for good. Egypt used to let us use her car to do our shit back in the day, and she was a rider for Drip, and he knew it, so let's hope he learned his lesson this time.

Louve would be pissed if she found out I was in the trap counting this money up and weighing the product. I wasn't cooking and cutting shit up, but she wouldn't be any happier if she knew there were females here in only G-strings doing that job for me. I told her I had some business to handle but never stated what that exactly was. I talked to Edge and let him know everything was straight at the trap, and he invited me to come hang out and have a quick drink at the Gentleman's Cove. I decided to take him up on that offer. It was the perfect opportunity to get his input on a few business ventures and also to show him the ring I got for Louve. I loved her with everything in me, and I was ready to give her my last name. I made a few more rounds by some of the other traps and then slid off to the strip club.

I walked in and was escorted right over to the private section that

Edge had. He had a crew of his boys with him and a plethora of bad bitches dancing for them. I stopped one of the diamond bikini-clad waitresses and got me my own bottles of D'usse and sat back to enjoy the show. The waitress came right back with my bottles, and I slid her a dub as a tip. She winked and was on her way. I was a taken man, but I could look, and shorty's ass was drumming to its own beat as she walked away. I had to get my head together before I fuck around and slip up tonight.

BEFORE I KNEW it was beyond fucked up off them bottles. I stumbled my way to the bathroom off our VIP section and took a long ass leak. I sobered up a little bit during that time, and once I was done, I headed back out. I was almost at the stairs leading to our section when I was grabbed from behind by some soft hands. I turned to see miss beautiful bottle girl that waited on me earlier. I didn't even get to speak before her hands were inside my barely zipped and buckled jeans. She released the beast from my pants and stroked it with the precision and the perfect rhythm, and all I could do was fall back into the side of the railing for support. It was pitch black where we were, and the only light was from the row of lights lighting up each stair that lead to the level of VIP sections.

She dropped her sexy ass down into a squatting position, and all I saw was that big round ass lit up from the lights of the stairs under her and reflecting off the diamond bikini she wore. She was still stroking my brick hard dick with the perfect rhythm that caused my toes to tighten together inside my Yeezy's. She kept that going while she began to suck on the head slowly swirling her tongue around the tip. She suctioned each inch in and out until I was down her throat. The head was so lethal that after a few times of her humming, I was releasing a load down her throat. She swallowed every drop before standing up still stroking me keeping me hard as Chinese arithmetic. She turned around and started twerking making her ass clap and ripple in waves. She propped a leg up on the second to last step and slowly inserted a finger inside her pussy causing a trickle of her wetness to run down the inside of her thigh.

I lost all sense and for the first time in damn near seven years I was risking my relationship and about to cheat on my girl. In the beginning, I was young as hell and so was Louve, so I dipped out here and there, but eventually, there was no need or reason to. However, right here right now, I had to feel this shit in front of me. When I arrived, I placed a few condoms in my pocket as I entered VIP. I never thought I would really use them shits because typically I would just put them back on my way out, but grabbing a few became a habit from years of being in this spot. I tore the pack open still watching as she fingered fucked her wet sloppy center in front of me. I slid the magnum on and removed her hand. I put the head at the opening and knew this shit was about to be good. I slid in a bit more, and it gripped my shit like a too tight glove.

She started twerking causing me to slam deeper into her, and I gripped on to her ass tightly as I gave her hard deep strokes. She was bucking and moaning loud, but the music and noise drowned her out. I almost let off again when she started clamping her pussy muscles tightly on me. I made her bend over and gripped her ankles as I knocked the bottom out of her. She started cumming and squirting causing me to let off in the condom. I pulled out, and although I felt good as hell after hitting that bomb ass pussy that she was toting around, I had a wave of regret hit me as I gathered myself to head to the bathroom.

She passed me her number on a napkin and headed to the ladies bathroom. I looked at the number and her name Naomi written in cursive with a heart on the I. I shook my head and slid the used condom wrapper and the napkin with the number in my back pocket.

I cleaned myself up and splashed some water on my face. I checked my phone, and it was damn near three in the morning, so I decided it was time to call it a night. I said peace to my niggas and told Edge that I'd get up with him later. He was a wild ass nigga, and all I could do was shake my head because I was just on the same shit.

He had two of the strippers 69'n each other while another was topping him off right in the VIP. Yea, it was definitely time that I took my ass home to avoid doing anything else fucked up. I ain't know how to feel after doing that shit, so on my drive, I smoked a blunt to mellow myself out.

I arrived home a little after 3:30 and everyone was sound asleep. I went to my man cave to shower good and get changed into some gym shorts for bed. I tossed my clothes in my hamper taking a mental note to wash this hamper of towels and workout shit myself before Louve made her way down here to do them. I made my way upstairs and climbed right into bed with my baby. I felt like shit as I laid there and with her snuggled up on me now. I had to chill before I messed up a good thing. I had a woman I never had to ask to do anything because she was already doing it. We had our issues, but we got through those issues, so for the life of me, I had no clue why I fucked that girl because my baby had the best pussy I ever had, and it was literally all mine and had only been mine.

A night to ask her brother for his permission to marry his sister and show him the ring I picked out turned into me cheating on my girl. The guilt was eating at me like a motherfucker as I laid in this bed. I would have to hold off on this proposal until I figured out why I suddenly had the urge and temptation to cheat on Louve, and more importantly why I followed through with it. Sex was just sex, but it was something that pulled me in to actually fuck Naomi, and the fucked-up part is I was thinking about her right now and how I wanted to do that shit again. This shit was all kinds of bad. They say with more money comes more problems, and that shit was holding true right about now.

13

TORI

I was skeptical about this trip to Mexico that Edge planned for everyone and something inside told me this was more than a couple's getaway. See the ladies were green to the stuff they men did, but me, I had played a role in his drug empire a time or two. There were times I'd accompany Edge to close a deal or times I'd do money pickups out of state, so I knew exactly what my man was into, but Edge promised to slow down so that we could have a family. I refused to give him a baby while he was knee deep in the streets. When he went legit with the weed that we would soon be owning a dispensary for, then I'd give him a baby, oh and when I have a ring too.

I was out shopping for this Mexico trip. I was strolling by a little bistro that has outdoor tables and chairs, so I decided to stop in and grab lunch. I stood in line and ordered my stuff to go. I waited off to the side for my number to be called. I was scrolling through my phone on Instagram when I had to do a second scroll backwards to see if my eyes were seeing what was real. This local Instagram model Rockai I follow leaked a picture of her holding onto a man's huge penis through his jeans. The only reason I did a double back on the post and scrolled up to again was that the hand in the picture was looking too familiar. Low and behold there was Edge's hand tatted all up with my name in the mix of those tats in clear view holding his signature cigar from his personal collection line of cigars. I was hurt, but I was madder because I thought we finally passed the cheating and hoes. I had a little trick for him though. Two can play this game, and it was time to tango.

My number was called, so I grabbed my food and headed out to my car around the block. I no longer had an appetite and was busy thinking of my next move and my plan for this situation. I was so deep in thought that I walked right into a firm ripped up sweaty chest dropping my phone and bags. My soup spilled out its container and onto the ground. I dropped down in a squat to pick up my things, and the body I had run into came down with me and helped me. Once we had everything up, I was about to apologize and leave, but this man was so fine that he had me speechless.

"Sorry about that, lil mama. I was on my phone leaving out the gym right here and walked into you. But shit, I'm glad I did. You are fine as fuck. Excuse my French, but you are beautiful."

He talked directly to my face and not my breasts like most men. This man was so fine.

"It's cool. I was about to apologize to you because I wasn't paying much attention either and bumped into you," I quietly said, feeling butterflies fly through my stomach. *What the hell was going on right now?*

"Well at least let me replace your lunch," he replied, walking towards the bistro without waiting for me to even decline.

What's the worst that can happen from a harmless lunch?

IT HAD BEEN a few days since I met Saga, and he occupied all of my free time that Edge left me with. Lord, that man was fine as hell, and his name alone had me enticed. We talked all day and night about any and everything, and we had plans to get up after my trip to Mexico. I'd been keeping my game face on with Edge and playing nice, even though I was pissed at him. I planned on getting more info on this chick while on this trip because he was too cozy with her in that picture for it to be a random fling. I was at a fork in the road on our relationship because, after all this time, he was still playing. And now here I was entertaining the next nigga's calls and texts, but mainly because I was lonely and wanted to do the same shit he did, except this thing with Saga seemed a little deeper than I anticipated.

We had sexual tension that I was avoiding after a conversation we had the other night about the way he would he be eating my pussy if I was in his tub instead of my own. He had tried to get me over that night, and it almost worked until Edge came home earlier than expected drunk and high. We had some bomb ass sex, but I thought about Saga's word and his deep voice the whole time and the images of his rock-hard abs and the long thick slightly curved dick pictures he had sent to me. He was a true stereotype walking— a sexy, fine as hell black nigga with a big dick that all girls dream about. I knew I was in for some shit the minute he got his hands on me. Saga had a baby mother, but he claimed they were just co-parenting. I told him he didn't have to lie about anything to me because I had Edge and didn't plan on leaving him anytime soon or if at all.

The fact was, I loved Edge, I loved him to death, but I was just tired of his shit. The lies the games, the streets, and lonely nights were taking a toll on me. I was gone have me a little fun too. He wouldn't be the only one that was living their best life. If he wanted to act single cool, we would both do that with ease. That's all Saga was to me just some fun on the side, and a good time or two to get my turn at testing the waters. I had no plans on actually doing anything other than flirting with him and maybe let him take me out to lunch again. As far as sex, I don't know if I had it in me to step out there and actually have sex with someone other than Edge.

Mexico

We had just settled in at the resort and Edge was already on the phone making business plans and arranging meetings. We were not even here a damn day, and he was already about to be ghost. I fucking knew it was too good to be true that we get to have a week of just us time and bond. I was already annoyed with him, so I decided to go hang out with Louve and Egypt. Louve texted me ranting about Kilo leaving her with the kids and going to meet with Edge about business. I had spotted a kid's club open twenty-four hours for parents. We were going to check them in, and then do our own thing. I had seen a spa and a bar, and I figured we could hit the beach and local shopping stands.

Louve was so happy to drop the kids off. Even though she couldn't drink with me and Egypt, she was still able to hang and enjoy some much-needed freedom. Kilo was off doing business with Edge and Drip, so that left her hands full with the kids so this opportunity to drop them off is like a gift from Tiffany's to her. I left her to check the kids in and went to get us a Cabana on the beach. I ran into Egypt as I was cashing out for our private VIP cabana with a personal bottle girl. It was time to turn up and have a good time with or without our men.

"Hey, Egypt boo, what's up with you? You look shocked or scared like you saw a damn ghost," I inquired, eyeing her.

"I just saw my ex, and I kind of dipped and ghosted him a few years ago after I met Drip. I took off with the engagement ring pawned and used the money to move to California from Florida, I don't know if he saw me, but he will probably start some shit if he does," she replied, pulling her sun hat down and securing her shades over her eyes.

"Oh damn, well if you spot him, point him out so that I can help you stay low key and out of his sight," I responded as I undid my sarong and laid on the lounger in our cabana.

"Maybe I'm just tripping. Maybe it was someone who looked like him," she replied with much uncertainty.

Egypt finally relaxed, and we sipped away on frozen margaritas, and Louve had made it over to join us and drink her virgin daiquiris. We had a blast just laughing and having girl time until the sun went down. The bar area started to turn up and was playing some good music. I decided to stay behind and drink a little more before heading to the room to get dressed. We all were supposed to have our own date night tonight with our guys, and I had no clue where Edge and I were going tonight, but I was ready to get some alone time with my man. I missed the way Edge, and I was when he first snatched me up at eighteen. Edge used to make time for me all the time and never had me feeling the way that I do now.

14

EDGE

We walked into the private conference room of the business office at the resort hotel. I sat at the head of the table on one end with Drip on my left and Kilo on my right. I checked my Rolex. We were on time, but the Dons were not, which was odd because they ain't play about arriving on time, especially with how busy they were. No sooner than I was about to make a call to one of the Dons workers who handled the scheduling of these meetings, three guys rolled in dressed to the nines in Hugo Boss, but the street in them was evident. I looked to my niggas to see if they knew who these niggas were, but they were just as confused as I was. I stood to my feet, hands behind my back close to my nine in my waistband, and then finally the one who I guess was the ringleader spoke up.

"You can relax my nigga. We ain't on no beef. Shit, we're here to talk business and get to the money. I'm Saga. The Don Cortez sent me. He had a family emergency to tend to. This is my boys Fresh and Roof," he stated while taking a seat at the opposite end directly across from me. His flunkies followed him, sitting on each side of him.

"Don Garcia, Lopez, and Cortez ain't mentioned shit about you to me, so I'ma make a call to get to the bottom of shit before I shoot first, never ask a question, just go on about my day, and get some pussy," I replied, picking up my cell and making a call.

"Do what you need to, man. I got pussy to get to as well, some good ass pussy too, matter of fact the best I ever had, so you are wasting more time than necessary when we could be on our way already to the ladies we have waiting. Let's get to these numbers and get business moving," he said as he proceeded to pull out a cigar and light it. He slid a folder across the table to me.

It was something about this nigga Saga that I didn't like and didn't trust. I wasn't feeling his whole vibe at all. The nigga was fake as they come. I had to hit up my PI to get the real on this Ronald McDonald clown. I disconnected the call and entertained the information he passed along from the Dons.

We talked numbers and got down to a concrete deal that would have me sitting back stacking money by the minute. I saw the wheels turning in Kilo and Drip's heads, and I knew from the look in their eyes that they were hungry to get shit poppin'. My team was full of real hittas, and we were about to take Englewood and the rest of Cali by storm. I may have been moving up in this game, but I had plans for the community too.

We exited the meeting official bosses in direct business with the Dons and shit was squared away early, so I decided we needed to celebrate, but I wanted to show my appreciation to the guys, so I led them to this private side of the resort where the strip club was something they had never experienced before. We entered Pleasure Paradise and were led straight to VIP. I planned to live a little tonight and spend the rest of the trip with my baby Tori. I had been neglecting her, and I knew she was fed up with my shit. However, I'd be back in her good graces first thing tomorrow morning when we spent all day together. I had a treat planned for her.

The music was bumpin', and all the strippers were topless or engaged in the wet t-shirt competition. We had liquor flowing heavy, and I was on one smoking on my blunt and enjoying the scenery. I let my mind wander to Tori and decided to head back to the room and make up for the time lost lately instead of waiting until the morning.

My baby had been patient with me, and it was time I got on my shit with her.

"Yo Drip, Kilo, I'm out. See y'all boys in the morning for the jet skis. Be safe and stay out of trouble," I said, slapping hands with them before exiting VIP and then heading out the door.

It took me a while to make it to the front because females in this business knew money when it was in their presence, and they were throwing themselves at me for a shot to dance privately for me.

I walked in the main entrance instead of our private back entrance so that I could stop by the gift shop and grab a few things for Tori. On my way to the gift shop, the front desk worker stopped me and gave me an envelope and a room key. I thanked her and smiled as I opened the letter. I assumed it was from Tori planning something sexy for me, but to my surprise, it was Rockai, my on again off again side piece. She knew her place for the most part, but once she started catching feelings, I cut her back. I ran into a few weeks back, we hung out after that, and things started back up. I had no emotional connection to her. It was just sexual attraction mixed in with the skills she had that allowed shit to always get poppin' between us.

I was curious as to why she chose to make her way to the resort when I set her up at a completely different one as reinforcement for this deal. Rockai did work for me here and there mostly as arm candy to seal a deal, and that's why I brought her along this go around because if needed, she would help close the deal with the Dons. With the deal being closed, I was planning to send her back to Cali first thing in the morning. I guess I can get a nut for the road because I was ending this shit with her. Tori was worth me being faithful and committing to her like she deserved. I reached the room and let myself in.

On the bed was a butt naked and very sexy Rockai waiting for me. She climbed off the bed and swayed her sexy ass over to me. I was in a trance watching her titties bounce with each step she took. She grabbed my hand and led me to the couch where I took a seat and got comfortable. Rockai knew what I liked and just want I expected from her. I loved for a female to strip dance and make that ass clap for me. It was an obsession of mine. The shit was like a form of art, and it was one reason I decided on opening a few strip clubs of my own.

Rockai danced for me and got me hard as a brick watching her twerk while in a split. I picked her up and carried her to the back of the villa to the bedroom. Entering the room, there was a sexy Latin chick lying in bed. I looked to Rockai who had a devious smirk on her face. I watched as they gave me a show, and I knew I'd be here a while.

15

TORI

I had been back in the room now for over two hours waiting on Edge, and I was over it. His ass never ceased to amaze me. We were in Mexico, and he was still doing the same shit he did at home. I could have kept my ass at home and had some fun with Saga instead of this lonely ass trip. My girls were out with their men enjoying the night, and I was here waiting on this dumb ass nigga. Nope, not any longer, I was taking my ass to the bar for some fun. Here I was dressed, looking good, horny as hell on a beautiful resort, and I still end up alone while my man is here.

Shit had I known this was what it would be like, I would have just planned a ladies trip. I grabbed my clutch and headed over to the front of the resort to catch a shuttle to this club that I had seen a flyer for a party tonight.

I arrived at the club and went straight to the bar to order a drink. I sat on the stool and flagged over the bartender. She smiled and gave me the one-minute finger signal and finished the orders at the end of the bar. Another bartender returned, I guess from break, and she started working the other end of the bar. I shook my head getting irritated that I sat in the middle away from the crowd of people at the bar, which I now see why they were on the ends where the bartenders were stationed. The bar was packed, and drinks were flowing heavy throughout the club.

The bartender I flagged early came over and placed a margarita with a corona shooter in front of me. I told her I didn't order this, and she told me the guy at the end sent it over to me. I followed her finger pointing to the direction she had just come from, and my eyes fell on Saga. My mouth dropped, and he signaled for me to come over. I grabbed my drink and headed to the side he was at. I took a seat taking in his cologne that had me ready to jump on him. He told me he was here on business, and I gave him a side eye hoping that he wasn't a stalker. He told me that he didn't tell me he would be here for that exact reason because he didn't want to scare me off.

We laughed, drank, and danced for hours, and before I knew it, we were in a corner damn near fucking. I broke away from his lips and removed his hands from my ass pulling my dress down. I knew what I wanted to do, and the moment of truth would come once I checked my phone. I pulled my phone out from my clutch, and I had not one missed call or text from Edge. I did, however, have a text from Kilo advising me that Edge told him to let me know he was ok, he had to handle some more business on another part of Mexico and would be back in the morning.

I didn't believe that shit at all, and it was ok because I had one more way to know what I suspected was real. I went to Instagram and what do you know, Rockai was in Mexico at a resort not too far from here. I powered my phone off, tossed it in my bag, and grabbed Saga's hand getting his attention from his phone. I mouthed to him that I needed him now. He knew exactly what I was saying, and we left the club hand in hand. He led me towards an awaiting limo. We headed back to his private beach house.

I was in awe as we pulled up to this glass and white beach house. It was breathtaking and looked like something off TV.

Saga led the way, and once inside, I was even more in awe. This house was so big and decorated beautifully. I wondered if his wife had a hand in it. I had researched Saga, and I knew he had a wife and kids, but right now, I didn't care because I had a cheating ass man that I loved that I wasn't leaving. I wanted attention, I wanted sex, and I wanted to feel wanted. Saga was always telling me how sexy I was, how good I looked and smelled, and how he wanted to taste me. Things were things Edge used to always say to me, and now we barely say a word to each other. For me to get time with Edge, I have to do pop-ups on him and hope that he don't have a bitch or a dead body there.

I never once stepped out on Edge, but he'd also had never been how he is now. I was pulled from my thoughts by the sensual kisses that Saga placed to my neck from behind me. Saga began to unbutton my sheer shirtdress. He removed the sheer dress and then the thin slip I wore under it. I stood in his foyer in my heels, bra, and lace boy shorts as he circled me admiring my body. I was feeling the many margaritas that I had, and I began to take off my bra. I dropped it and attempted to get my boy shorts off, but he had swooped me up and carried me to the back of the home and into the open double French doors.

Saga tossed me on the bed and stepped out of his clothes. I was damn near ready to get up and put my clothes back on when I saw the girth and length he was working with. He must have sensed my hesitation because he ripped my boy shorts off and began to eat me as if I was his last meal. The pleasure I was feeling was outweighing the guilt I had a few moments ago, and before I could even come down off the high he gave me, he was flipping me over and stroking me from the back. Thoughts of Edge were gone, and all I was concerned with was the orgasm that was building inside me. Saga was holding me at no mercy, and I loved every minute of it.

Surprisingly no regrets crossed my mind, and I now understood how men could cheat feel no emotions and strictly just have sex. This type of sex was worth risking it all for. Saga moved things within me I never knew was there. It wasn't love at all, but it was good sex indeed.

16

KILO

The time in Mexico with Louve was needed, and I was happy to see her happy after the rough times we had. We had been back now for a few days, and the new roles we now had were in full swing. Today I was out early getting shit rolling and bringing our team up to speed on the changes and promotions within the crew. Muse wasn't feeling the way Edge was taking over, so he opted to keep his shit the way it was but with no hard feelings on Drip and me moving on to better things. He knew I wasn't around for the shit we used to do. After almost losing my life, I wasn't risking that for no one anymore. That shit was only gone last for so long, but he'd already made his decision, and we made ours.

I pulled up to the car wash and hopped out leaving my car with the detail guy. I decided to head across the way to this little Jamaican spot and grab some food while I waited on my whip. I entered the door and was greeted by a big chick with dreads. I placed my order and had a seat. I was scrolling on my phone browsing some sports highlights when a laugh caught my ear. I looked up to see Naomi coming through the door with a group of girls. I had to admit shorty was looking good, and I knew I shouldn't even be staring her down the way I was, but Naomi had some type of effect on me that I couldn't resist. When our eyes connected, she gave me that look that let me know she was just as happy I was to see me as I was to see her.

"You looking for me, beautiful?" I asked as I walked up to Naomi.

"Actually, I just came for lunch and got to see your handsome face as a surprise," she replied as she walked away to catch up to her friends.

"I ain't been able to get you and that pot of gold between yo legs out my head," I whispered in her ear and then placed a kiss in the space behind her ear. I felt her body shiver, and I knew she wanted me just as much as I wanted her.

"Damn, I been thinking about you too," she replied, turning to face me.

"My car will be ready across the street at the wash in fifteen minutes. I'll be back out front waiting for your sexy ass," I replied, and I placed a kiss to her hand and grabbed my order that had just been called and was out the door.

I didn't stop to think about what the hell I was about to do but instead, let my little head lead me right to my car and back out front waiting on Naomi as I promised. Her friends were eyeing me from the front of the restaurant where they all stood talking. Ten minutes passed, and finally, Naomi came over to the car and climbed in. I didn't even get a chance to ask her if we were heading to a hotel or her place before she told me her address. I jumped in traffic and was on the way.

Naomi propped her leg up on the dash and started fingering herself in the passenger seat. The noises that filled the car and her moans had me ready to pull over and take her in the car. She noticed the bulge and tent forming in my pants and wasted no time unleashing the beast and placing it in her mouth. I was in for a world of trouble, and I had no idea the storm coming my way from a few moments and pumps of pleasure.

17

LOUVE

The trip to Mexico was amazing much needed, and I had never been happier in my life. However, for some reason, I had a feeling that this happiness was short lived. I felt like a cloud was coming to rain on our parade.

I was home alone while the kids were at school, so I decided to get the laundry started. I loved having a second-floor laundry room. I didn't like the fact that the kids swim clothes and towels were always left downstairs for me to bring up. My kids were water babies and swam almost every day, so I knew the pile was probably big of towels. I made my way to the mudroom off the garage, and sure enough, the hamper was full. I remembered I hadn't done Kilo's gym laundry in a while, so I headed to his gym room in the basement to grab his hamper. I checked the bathroom before heading back up, and he had a pile of clothes in there too. I tossed those in and made my way upstairs to start the laundry.

The day was going by fast as I washed and folded the laundry putting everyone's things in their rooms. I loved being a housewife, but I knew I wanted more. I still hadn't told Kilo about the program letter I received, and I knew I had to do that soon. I was done with the kid's clothes and still had two hours before their bus arrived, so I moved on to me and Kilo's clothes.

I always checked his pockets because he had a habit of leaving weed blunts money and whatever else in his pockets. I empty the first few pairs of pants and found money and change totaling $300 that I decided I'd deposit in the savings account that I opened a few days ago. Now that things were on the up and up, it was time to be smart with our money and start adulting like we need to. I got to a pair of jeans that smelled of weed and Henny. I searched the front pockets and found the paper band from a stack 100 one-dollar bills and a few singles, so I knew it was from the strip club.

I checked the back pockets and found gum in one, and my heart dropped to the pit of my stomach when I pulled out a Magnum condom wrapper opened, empty, and clearly used, as well as a napkin from the Gentleman's Cove strip club with a name and number written on it. The tears started flowing, and I was heartbroken. For the first time ever, Kilo hurt me. I couldn't gather myself, so I laid there for some time just letting the tears fall. I did everything a woman is supposed to do, and yet he still cheated. I held him down when he was recovery and in rehab from almost dying, and he crossed me in the dirtiest way possible. The kids would be home soon, so I did what a mother does, and that was put on a strong front and fake it until you make it through the day.

THE KIDS CAME in like a storm talking about their day as we did homework, watched some TV, and then ate dinner before they were off to bed. I was still hurting and hadn't heard from Kilo, and I honestly wasn't looking forward to seeing him because I didn't know what I might do. I called up Tori and told her everything, and she was just as shocked and hurt like me. I told her I needed to go to NY and visit my dad and see about the program. She offered to get the kids and keep them for the weekend. She would pick them up from school, and I would take an Uber to the airport as soon as I got them on the bus.

I needed to clear my head, and this was the perfect time. It was never a time I ever thought there could be Louve and no Kilo because, from the day we met, it's been us and all about our kids and us. As it stands today for the first time I'm going to take a break and see how I feel about a life with no Kilo. That cloud feeling that I had from earlier confirmed that the good times don't always last. We had made many strides in the right direction, and Kilo throws a monkey wrench into our whole set up. I didn't even know how to approach the situation because I was certain that I'd end up laying hands and feet all over his dirty cheating ass.

I would never involve Edge in our shit, and because of that, Kilo is lucky because I was so ready to tell Edge about this nigga and his shit and watch him get his ass beat. Who am I kidding? Edge was probably there with Kilo doing Tori dirty too. The only time Kilo goes to the strip club is when he with Edge and Drip, so I'm sure the three blind mice were rolling together. Tori was better than me because I wasn't putting up with that shit like she did with my brother. I called up Kilo out of anger, and only got madder when his phone went to voicemail.

"You dirty ass dog, you promised never to do me foul Kilondre. Whatever bitch you fucked with that Magnum named Naomi, you might as well stay with her. Don't bring your ass to my house!" I screamed into the phone on his voicemail.

I never got a call back before I went to bed and that confirmed that we had reached the lowest point of our relationship ever. I just knew Kilo would have rushed home and let me know I had it all wrong, and shit even beg and plead for me to forgive his mistake, but I got nothing but unreturned calls and ignored text messages. I packed the kids up and dropped them off to Tori, and I went right to the airport in an Uber. I needed to get away, and I needed to get away immediately, or else shit was gone get real.

All the shit I had been through with this man, and he has lowered us to this. I'm sitting up here pregnant taking care of five people, not just me or my kids, but Kilo too. I cooked, I cleaned, and I washed too many damn clothes to be reduced to the baby mother that he chooses to cheat on. We weren't perfect, but our shit was solid, or so I thought. You can give a man your kidney, and they'd a still entertain another female.

18

TORI

I was stuck in this dilemma, and I had no clue how to get out of it. The worst part was I was yearning to feel Saga, and I had no business even thinking about him. After what went down in Mexico, I told myself that was it, and I would never talk to him again. But, that was a lie because the first time Edge ran off with that bitch, and I was sure it was her, then I was running off to be with Saga.

Tonight was no different. As I rode the elevator up to his loft, I decided that tonight was it. I had to gain control before this all turned bad. I was sleeping with my man's connect, and that was all bad. Edge would kill us both and not think twice about it. I had seen firsthand the way Edge handled people who do him wrong, and I wanted no parts of that monster. Things with Edge were still off, and I was feeling lonelier than I ever have before.

Saga had let the cat out the bag when he heard me say Edge's name, and I damn near shit my pants when he told me. This was too close to home and too risky to be doing. I enjoyed the dick, but I lived my life more, and no sex was that good to lose my life for it. Things had been crazy with my life watching the kids for those few days after Louve left until Kilo came and took them home. He begged me to tell him where she was, and he told me all about the voicemail that she left him, but that was my best friend. I could never rat her out. Even if I felt a little sorry for Kilo, I had to have Louve's back. Egypt and I had been hanging more than before, but tonight I just used her as an alibi in case Edge asked. Egypt said she was on board and had my back with the story and that it helped her out too because she had something to handle as well and didn't need Drip to know her real whereabouts. I made a mental note to get all the details from her on that later.

I reached the door and rang the bell patiently waiting as I heard Saga making his way to the door. I came prepared to make the last time count. Saga opened the door in nothing but a pair of Nike sweat shorts and a bottle of 1738 in his hand. The tattoos that were scattered about his torso were on full display. He was most definitely a sight to see, and if I didn't have Edge, he'd be a full entree on my menu, but for now, I'd take this snack. I stepped into the loft letting Saga by to lock the door behind me. I untied my Michael Kors black trench coat letting it fall to the floor, exposing my bare ass in my black, La Perla lace thong. I wore no bra and my black red bottoms.

I felt Saga's eyes on me, so I turned my head slightly to look over my shoulder, and just as I figured, he was watching me with so much lust in eyes as he bit his lip and held onto tight to that nine-inch anaconda between his legs. I decided to kick things off as this would be the last time. Strutting over to his entertainment center I connected my iPhone to his Bluetooth speaker and put on my Trey Songz mix. The first song was "Last Time" and that was perfect for this occasion. Making way to the kitchen, I climbed up on the island, and I laid across it sexily playing with my nipples, watching Saga as he watched me. Saga took a sip from his bottle and set it beside me. His strong hands graced my neck before roughly grabbing me by it pulling me up to kiss me.

We kissed sloppily as his hand roamed all over my body. Before I could assist him with removing my thong, he snatched it off ripping it in two. He brought it to his nose sniffing it and closing his eyes as if I was the best thing he ever smelled. I used my hands to pull his shorts down enough to free the beast that I was here for. He slapped my hands away and pushed me back on the cool, granite island top. My body was on fire, and the coolness of the counter created a euphoric rush throughout me. Saga stroked himself for me to see, and the veins that popped out let me know he was harder than a steel beam. I spread my legs wide letting him see how wet I was, anticipating him inside me. I used my middle finger to dip inside my honey pot and bring it to his mouth where he licked and slurped at it like it was dipped in pure honey.

That was enough to send him over the edge because he dived face first sending me on an orgasmic chase, the high I'd been craving since the night we first headed into this forbidden territory of lust and deceit. I rocked my hips and grind my pelvis into his face and tongue loving the way he was handling his business. Saga was a beast with his mouth, and I knew I had to let this go before I get too far gone. He stopped as I was almost at my peak, and my eyes shot open. Saga was smiling with a devilish grin on his face, and I looked on in hunger as he slid a Magnum XL on his rock-hard dick. That first thrust after he slid in sent us into a fuck session that lasted way longer than I had planned.

A FEW HOURS LATER, I was laid across his couch trying to gather myself after falling asleep. I retrieved my phone, and it was well after three a.m., and I had multiple missed calls from Edge and Louve. I thought quick on my feet and shot Louve a text that I caught Edge cheating, and that's why I disappeared for a few hours to clear my head. I knew she would pass that on to Edge and just as I expected like clockwork, as I was tying my trench coat up and getting my things together, the apology texts from Edge came flooding in. I also shot a quick text to Egypt to check in on her, but she never responded. I was only out doing me because I knew what Edge was on, but I was ready to stop the games and get our shit together. I went in search of Saga and found him smoking a blunt on his balcony.

"Hey you, I'ma get going, and although this has been good and fun, it has to stop. I'ma fall back. It's time to cut off communication before things get complicated." I started watching him waiting for his response. He remained quiet, and then he started to laugh like I just told the funniest joke.

"Yo, shut the fuck up with that shit, ma. You trying to cut a nigga off for real?" he replied as he stepped in my face letting the smoke from his Kush blow past my nose.

"First of all, don't be telling me to shut the fuck up, and second, nigga you work too close to my man, and you have a wife, not just a baby mother. Yea nigga, I know all about her and the three kids, and it's all good. We had fun, and it's time to let it go," I replied with attitude, crossing my arms as I waited for him to speak.

"Bitch, I love you! It ain't that simple, so go on home to your *man*, if he's even there, and we'll plan our next meet up. Drive safe." He kissed my forehead and headed inside his loft and to his room.

I was stuck on stupid and at a loss for words. This man really thought he had it like that. Oh well, he'll learn the hard way. I'm not fucking with him. His ass is crazy. Who even says some shit like that to someone like it's normal? I grabbed my keys and stormed out, letting the door slam hard behind me. Thanks to Saga I was butt ass naked under this trench coat and would need to put on my clothes from my gym bag in my trunk. I took my time getting home, and of course Edge wasn't home but knowing him he was out at every hotel looking for me.

I rushed inside and showered and then threw on a nightgown and was in bed. I had a text from Saga telling me not to try no shit and that he loves my ass. I blocked his number and deleted the texts. I knew I had to because he was doing too much now. I just hope he lets it go and keeps shit cool, but my gut told me shit was about to get really bad.

19

EDGE

I had been having a bad vibe with this nigga Saga, so I had my PI follow him and get some information for me on what exactly he was into. What I wasn't expecting was for my PI to be placing photos of Tori leaving from hotels with this nigga in front of me. At first, I was thinking she was setting me up, but then I realized this was personal. She was fucking this nigga. I had a little surprise for her and her side nigga the next time they decided to meet up. I knew Tori was tired of my shit and the cheating, but a nigga never thought in a million years she would step out on and with my connect. I was .38 hot and ready to kill both they asses for crossing me like I was some sucka ass nigga.

Tori was out here really entertaining the next nigga. My bitch had a side nigga. What was the world coming to? I shook my PI's hand thanked him for his work on this and placed all the photos and documents in the folder and headed out to my car. I needed to smoke some real shit to calm my nerves, so I fired up the special batch that I had left over from Mexico and let it soothe me as I inhaled it. I sat for a while thinking on my next move, and I knew exactly what needed to be done. It was gone hurt a few people, but that's the price you pay for disloyalty.

I sent a text to Kilo and Drip and let them know we needed an emergency meeting ASAP at my hideaway in Calabasas. I pumped some Jagged Edge *J.E. Heartbreak* and rode out to my destination.

"YOU SURE ABOUT THIS SHIT, Edge? Kilo asked, looking over the documents and pictures that I had received from the PI.

"For real though, maybe you are jumping the gun with this plan," Drip said while standing in the back corner with his arms crossed like he was standing guard.

I stayed quiet just looking between the two of them before speaking. I wasn't mad at them, so I had to check myself before I spoke so that it didn't come off wrong to them. They knew how I felt about loyalty, so this was a no brainer in my eyes.

"I know there will be some backlash behind this, but it's a necessary move, and I already have things set in motion, so let's move on to the next course of business because that's literally a dead issue." I sipped on my D'usse on the rocks and got the rest of the meeting going.

After all was discussed that was imperative and necessary, we parted our ways.

I wasn't ready to face Tori, so I decided to stay at my hideaway spot for the night. As a man, you never expect to feel so hurt, but the shit was tearing a nigga like me with a ruthless ass heart down. We can dish some shit out, but we damn sure can't take it. I had taken Tori through some shit but damn you don't get a nigga back like this. I wasn't even in the mood to entertain any of the chicks that were blowing me up or even Rockai who was currently sending me all types of enticing pictures trying to get me to bite the bait. Normally she'd be here laid up with me, but that shit got me sitting here nursing this drink with a broken heart. That shit sounds weak as hell to me, but it's the truth and the shit I was gone have to do was about to create a whole lot of static.

I picked up my ringing cell and almost answered for Tori, but I refused to fall into that shit. I had to follow through with my plan and talking to her would only complicate shit and get me off my square. The thing about me is that once I set my mind on something as deep as taking a motherfucker out, I follow through with it. I didn't want to see Tori until it was time to get this shit going in motion. I called my sister up for the thousandth time and got sent to the voicemail. I don't what the hell was going on with Louve ass, but I'm gone blame it on the pregnancy and the shit she is going through with Kilo. I tried to stay out they shit but I was pissed to find out he hurt my sister, but I couldn't talk after the shit I'd done Tori plus I was still on bad terms with my little sister for pulling Kilo back into this street life.

"I know yo bald headed ass see me calling you. I need to make sure you straight LouLou and curse yo silly ass out for leaving my nieces and nephew. This is not even like you. Lou, you're the best mother I know. Call me back, apple head. I love you," I spoke into the phone, leaving her a voicemail.

I was stressed the hell out behind the two girls I loved the most, and it was time for my ass to go to bed. I showered to try to de-stress and relax, but all I saw was the photos of Saga and Tori, and that had me ready to go out murk both they asses at this very moment. So much for relaxing and de-stressing, that shit was a dub. I laid my ass in bed but ass naked just thinking on my next moves, staring out my huge picture window at the skyline, and that helped me to relax, so I knew sleep wasn't far.

20

KILO

I was losing my mind not knowing where Louve was at, but I know it's all my fault. Tori told me she was safe and would be home soon, but that was it. She left me that one voicemail and then blocked my ass from calling texting, Facebook, Instagram, and Snapchat. She was on straight bullshit with me. She was out here pregnant with our child and ran off to who knows where without telling me shit. The kids were sick of me too because I couldn't do shit like they mama. KJ done screw faced me more than a few times, but I'ma let him have that because he looks up to me, and he loves his mama. So to see that I fucked up with his mama, the one that I'm always teaching him to respect and treat her like a queen, makes it so that he ain't feeling his old man right now.

I had just got them all off to school and was heading to collect money and do drops. I was missing Louve something crazy and kicking my own ass for slipping up like that, and the fact that I doubled back was no better. While my dumb ass was out cheating, the love of my life was leaving my ass because of it. I now had to hire a nanny because I had too much shit to do, and I needed to be able to leave my kids with someone. Usually, it was Tori, but she's been busy and now I know why. I'd probably kill Louve ass if she ever cheated on me, so I couldn't blame Edge for the way he was feeling. I don't know how shit is about to play out, but disloyalty and being a snake isn't acceptable from anyone.

I was getting messages after messages from Naomi, but after the trouble that fucking with her caused, I was no longer interested, so I blocked her number and ignored all her attempts at trying to get up for the D. She was bad as hell, I couldn't deny that, but she wasn't shit compared to Louve, and sitting here sick missing her, I realize exactly what I have in her. I took my anger out on Louve a lot because I felt like my back was against the wall and less of a man when I was unable to provide how they needed me to. I threw us back into this fast life, and I fucked up instead of staying focus and faithful. I had to make this shit right, and if I knew where she was, I'd be on my way to do just that.

Egypt was sending me her childhood nanny Mrs. Lolly for the kids, so I had to get a move on it and meet her before the kid's bus came. I prayed this lady was good and would fit in with our family because the girls needed a granny figure considering neither of my and Louve's mamas was around or would ever be for that matter.

I pulled up to the last trap I had to hit and immediately that felt like something wasn't right. I watched from a few houses down as SWAT came from the back of an abandoned house and went straight to the front door of our trap. Now, the crazy shit is this has only been our trap since after Saga passed this territory to us. He needed it to be properly handled because the crew he had over here got caught with sticky fingers and were now pushing up daisies.

I snapped a few pictures and counted my blessings that I wasn't inside when this shit popped off. I did a U-turn back the other way and sent the pictures to Edge and Drip. Shit was getting real, and I knew Saga was behind this shit. He either set this up hoping to catch one of us up, or he knew they were watching this spot and never put us on. Either way, he was foul and out of pocket for this shit. We knew he seemed fake as hell when we met him, and I have a feeling he has a personal vendetta with Edge. He has to know who Tori belongs to. Shit, all of Cali knows that, so it's no excuse for fucking with your client's woman. I also had a feeling the Dons had no clue what exactly Saga had going on.

I headed home to meet with Mrs. Lolly because the amount of time I was about to be spending out here cleaning and fixing this shit was about to increase tremendously. KJ was gone be the hardest to please, but hopefully, this goes smoothly. I rushed home to straighten up because getting the kids ready and off to school was hell this morning, and the house was a mess. I did a load of laundry, hung up the clothes that were all over the room, and put toys back in the toy box. Just as I was emptying the trash, the doorbell rang, and my cell chimed with a text. Edge was pissed about the shit that I sent to him and wanted to meet at his house in an hour.

I opened the door and was greeted by an older short black woman. She looked so familiar to me, and I had no idea why because I had never met her before. I went to shake her hand, but she hugged me instead. I led her to the living room, and we sat down to talk. I had to tuck a sock into the couch that was sticking out before she sat down. I offered her some coffee or water, but she declined. She stared at me, and I finally spoke up.

"Thank you for meeting with me. The children will be home in about twenty minutes so that you can meet them and get a better feel of them and their personalities," I stated before sipping my bottle water.

"Well, I run a tight ship when I nanny. Schoolwork and any activities they are involved in are priority. I offer cleaning, cooking, and taking the children out on trips. I also will take them to church for bible study on Sundays," she replied before pulling out a folder and handing it to me.

I was a bit taken aback at how bold this little old lady was, but I like her. I skimmed through the documents and was impressed with the reference forms and the contracted services agreement. I signed the documents and then handed them to her. She signed and gave me the second copy and kept one for herself. This was gone to be perfect for my kids and me. I just hope Louve won't mind because even when she returns, I'm keeping Mrs. Lolly on the payroll to help out, especially with a new baby on the way. I was wishing that into existence that Louve would return home and soon. I was giving her three days, and then I'm turning up the heat and pulling out all the stops to find her.

The kids' bus pulled up, and I went outside to get them and give them a prepping on Mrs. Lolly and the way to behave. KJ was quiet and headed in ahead of us as the girls told me about their day and asked for pizza for dinner because my cooking was bad. I just laughed them off and reminded them, especially the baby, Kailis. She be telling everything and asking a thousand questions. She really is her mama's child. She had no damn filter and would speak what came to her mind. I introduced the kids to Mrs. Lolly, and they all sat and talked for some time before the pizza arrived. After dinner, I showed Mrs. Lolly the guest room before I headed out to meet with Edge and Drip.

The kids seemed to take to Mrs. Lolly pretty well and the fact that she was an older black woman with that no-nonsense mentality, I knew my kids were in good hands. I was grateful that we found her, and it helps, but I want my woman home with her family where she belongs. Louve was the glue that held us all together. I was losing hope that we would get back on track and a part of me was scared she would eventually come get the kids and leave my ass here alone. That was enough to make any man who knew he was wrong to fix his ways and straighten up.

21

LOUVE

I was missing my kids and even Kilo's cheating ass, but I had some important shit to handle before I went back home. I had spent a few days in New York and went to visit my dad on my last day. He gave me a lot of knowledge and information and sent me to do as he requested in his letter. I also stopped by and registered for the art program I received the invite for, and I figured since its only two weeks long I'll see about making it a summer vacation for the family.

I was back in Cali, but I had important business to handle, so I checked into a hotel and stayed there for the night after my flight returned. I had met with my father's attorney this morning to get all the information to his legit businesses and accounts that the government had originally frozen during the case. Now that they were no longer frozen, he wanted me to get my mother off the street with the money he had stashed. I had researched some rehab centers and made my way to the address that my father gave me to find my mom.

I pulled up to the address, and it looked like an abandoned house with boarded windows and all. The street was a dead end and crack heads that more so resembled zombies roamed about. I got out of the car and went to the door knocking hard on the boarded door. I could hear talking and rustling around, and then the sound of another door opening could be heard. I peeked off the side of the porch and saw a lady who looked to be a little older than me hanging out the window of the screen door that had no screen in it scratching her arms and looking at me like I was an unwanted guest. I waved my hand to her and then went down the stairs to speak to her. Once I walked to the side, she came out looking me up and down. I was ready to turn around and leave, but I needed to find my mother.

"Hi, I'm looking for Loucille or Lucy, is she here?" I asked anxiously waiting.

"Lucy not here. She has been at Cedars Sinai Hospital for two days now. I checked on her last night. She got a bad concussion from the fall she had, but she's a tough cookie she'll be good," she replied, smiling and laughing showing off her toothless grin. She was missing about four teeth.

"Oh my god, thank you so much for the info!" I shouted as I ran off and hopped in my rental, heading to the hospital.

I really wanted to call Kilo, but I didn't have time for the drama. I needed to check on my mother. Tears poured down my face as I thought about the last time, I had seen her. The truth was I needed her, and I needed her bad. As a young mother, I wanted to have that bond we had when I was a kid. I pray that this trip to the hospital is a blessing in disguise.

I made it to the hospital in record time and headed inside to the receptionist desk. I was given my visitor slip and headed to the ICU floor. I was advised that my mother was in a medically induced coma from the head trauma. They told me she fell down a flight of stairs, but police believe there was foul play, and she may have been pushed.

I took a deep breath as I reached her room and said a prayer. I walked in and couldn't stop the tears. My mother's once flawless caramel skin was ashy all over and pale. Her hair was a tangled-up mess, and she had to be only a hundred pounds soaking wet. This wasn't the lady I knew. The lady I remember was who I loved watching brush her hair and put it in rollers at night, or the lady that take the time to moisturize her skin.

I stepped closer to her bed, and although she had lost weight and looked ran down, she still held that timeless beauty. I pulled up a chair and began my healing process right there at her hospital bedside. I poured my heart out and spoke my true feelings, and then I prayed for her and for us as a family. I told her about the kids and even about Kilo. I wanted to call him and Edge, but this was something I'd do on my own. I had been taken care of and spoiled by these men for long enough. I talked so much that I made myself tired and thirsty, but I decided the minute I got here that I would remain here by her side until she woke up and after.

I bonded with her nurses, and we laughed and talked through the whole shift. By shift change, they had set me up a nice area to lay down and be somewhat comfortable. I got comfortable and started reading part 2 to this series I was obsessed with. *Perfect Dreams & Hood Nightmares: A Deadly Love Affair* by A. Gavin. She was a dope ass new author with my favorite author's publishing company Mz. Lady P Presents. I was never disappointed with any book from this company. They always had some good books to get lost in.

22

EDGE

I had to spend a large amount of money to get rid of the problems Saga sent our way. Having them pigs on payroll always was the best way to get out of shit like this. I kept a lawyer and judge on retainer, and I never really worried about shit coming down on me. With this shit popping off, it only made me kick my plan into gear that much sooner. I was riding in a throwaway car following Tori to this nigga's house. I had been keeping my game face on, but keeping my distance so that I could get this shit handled. Tonight was the night that they would answer for the shit they had been doing behind my back. I had an app on Tori's phone that let me read her messages. One thing I was happy to know was that she was ignoring that nigga until he threatened to harm me and anyone close to her.

Tori finally agreed to meet him today, and the meetup spot was some gas station on Sepulveda Boulevard. The bad part of Englewood is where he sent my baby too, and her ass went and never came to me about this issue. But shit, I guess when you are living foul, you can't speak up unless you ready to dish out your dirt. Tori wouldn't be meeting Saga though. That was for damn sure. Their playtime was over. Kilo had some of his boys from the Hittas stationed at the gas station waiting to snatch Tori up, and Drip had that nigga Saga tied up and waiting on me at the warehouse. I had my video recorder ready too, and the minute I stepped in and showed this nigga my face, the camera would be rolling.

The Dons would never believe that Saga was out to cross them and take down their whole operation and make the organization his own. I needed proof when I brought this shit to them and proof to justify me murking the connect's son. My PI let me know that although Don Lopez raised Saga like his own after his father died, he was actually his son after an affair he had with Saga's mother. When her husband found out, he approached Don Lopez, and the Don killed him after he threatened him. The story Saga had was a cover-up, but I was sure he was doing all this now after somehow finding out the truth.

I walked into the warehouse and Drip was smoking a blunt while talking on the phone. He gave me a head nod and strolled off to side while I pulled up a chair and sat right in front of a knocked-out Saga. I snapped a few pics and then slapped him a few times to wake him up. When his eyes focused on me, he let a menacing laugh and a Jack-O-Lantern grin. Drip had done a number on him. I guess he needed to get a few hits in of his own. I was convinced that Drip was crazier than my nutty ass. He had done some shit that made me side eye his ass a few times. I had the cameras rolling, and the fun was about to begin.

"You know Saga I always knew I didn't like yo ass, and now I know why. It's because you a snake ass nigga!" I shouted, standing to my feet and delivering a kick to the chair he was tied up in sending him across the floor close by Drip.

"Nigga, fuck your Bruce Leroy ass in here doing karate kicks and shit. Man, get this shit over with," he replied while laying sideways with a look that made him appear unbothered.

"Shut yo stupid ass up!" Drip yelled, dragging him back over to me and leaving him on his side. That was perfect angling I needed for my chopping block position anyway.

"So you ready to die, huh? Why did you do it?" I asked kneeling so that I was in his face.

"DO WHAT? FUCK YO BITCH OR FUCK OVER THE DONS? HAHAHAHAHAHAHAA!" he screamed, laughing in my face.

This nigga was a joke, so I had all I needed from his ass. I turned and went to the table of machetes and grabbed my custom one with the 24K gold handle. I didn't even warn this nigga or Drip. I just swung the machete up and yelled, "Off with his head!" bringing it down and delivering a clean cut, causing his head to roll over to Drip whose back was turned rolling up another L. The head hit the back of his wheat construction Timbs with a thud.

"What the..." Drip yelled, jumping and turning around. His eyes following Saga's head at his feet and then went to the trail of blood and other matter over to me holding the machete.

I just shrugged my shoulder and dropped the machete. I went to my car to retrieve the new Chanel bag that I purchased for Tori as a gift and placed Saga's head inside as a bonus. I laughed to myself thinking of the look she will have when she see this nigga's head in her new bag.

"Yo nigga, yo ass is sick and twisted! Bahahahahhhaa!" Drip yelled out in laughter.

"Nigga, yo ass is just as sick so how you sound," I replied as I zipped the bag closed and snatched the blunt from Drip.

"Who the hell yells out off with his head though, bro?" Drip asked, giving me a side eye as I passed the blunt back to him.

"I always wanted to say that shit while doing that except I wanted to really have a motherfucker in one of those chopping block things," I stated, walking out with the bag to my car. I shot the clean-up crew a text and made my way to handle this other disloyal person.

"Make sure that those tapes get to the Dons, ASAP!" I shouted as I exited the warehouse.

～

I HAD FINISHED my second blunt before I got out to go into the house. I had the Hittas bring Tori to my Calabasas home that she knew nothing about. Tonight everything was being laid out though. It was time to get this shit over with. I didn't even have my key in the door, but I heard Tori inside going off, demanding that they call me now. I just shook my head and laughed because this girl was a trip. She gets caught up but in here tripping like she not in the hot seat behind her hot ass being a thot.

I entered the house and couldn't believe these niggas was allowing her to act a fool. This one little nigga Spruce was looking scared as Tori stomped around the house with a bat in her hand. She had my collector's item bat down off the wall and was breaking and destroying shit all through the house. I quickly dismissed these niggas and snatched the bat out her hand.

I locked up after they left and came in the living room to see that Tori had sat her crazy ass down on the floor and was just looking at me. She had her hair up in the bun that I loved on her because it showed her face in full. I let my eyes roam over the outfit that she had on, and I was getting bricked up looking her perfect perky breasts as they peeked out the bottom of her crop top. Show wore no bra and had her pretty feet on display. She eyed me up and had a smirk on her face as her eyes landed on the bulge in my pants.

"You can sit there looking sexy as hell with that smirk on your face, but when I bring your side nigga's head to you in one of your Chanel bags, I bet that shit will be wiped off," I stated as I adjusted my gloves never taking my eyes off her.

"You can do as you please, Edge. You don't scare me with that threat, love. I welcome that shit with open arms. I told you time and time again to stop playing with me because when I play back, I don't play fair. Now you mad that I did the same shit to you that you always do to me— boy bye with that shit hahahahaa. If you want to kill Saga cool, I'll help you. The nigga was becoming an issue anyway, so you'll be doing us both a favor. Just know though that your side bitch Kai will be handled. I got that all on my own," she replied before getting up and coming over to me.

She dropped to her knees and freed the beast in my pants. I

couldn't even say anything after that because shorty had my mind gone, and I was at a loss for words. When her warm mouth slurped me up whole, all the shit that I talked about killing her ass was gone. The only thing getting killed tonight other than her side nigga was that pussy.

WE WENT AT IT, like some dogs in heat, all through the night until the wee hours of the morning. I let her get my ass with that, but I still had a surprise in the trunk for her. I had just showered and thrown on my clothes getting ready to handle this situation with the Dons. I had to fly out in a few hours with Drip and Kilo. I retrieved the special gift and placed it in a gift bag with tissue paper along with *I'm sorry* and *I love you* balloons. I woke Tori up with kisses all on her neck and lips. She stirred awake and smiled at me kissing me back deeply. I loved the fuck out this girl, and she knew that shit too. I had to love her ass to let her get away with this shit.

"I got you a few gifts, so get up and come to the kitchen," I said, leaving her and heading downstairs.

She came down after about fifteen minutes in my robe looking like a model. I pulled her chair out, and she sat down smiling wide at the food in front of her. I could cook breakfast quite well, so I went all out with a full spread for her. I handed her the largest gift bag first and sat down to watch her open it. She smiled wide and then pulled all the tissue paper out before she saw the bag inside. She started bouncing around all happy in her seat pulling the bag out. She had a confused look when she realized it had some weight to it, so she sat it on the table and then unzipped it.

"What the fuckkk? Oh my god Edge what the hell is wrong with you?" she shrieked out loudly with trembling hands as she looked into Saga's face in horror.

"You were loving that nigga's head down in my pussy, right? Let this be a warning of the lengths I will go to for what is mine. You belong to me Tori, and don't forget that shit again. Next time your sexy ass won't be able to stop me from killing you right along with any nigga that touches mine." I pulled her into my lap, and she just looked at me with a nervous expression as she bit her lip.

"Your ass is certified crazy. You ruined a $2,000 bag to prove a point," she said, looking at the bag and then back to me.

"Don't worry I got you another one in the car, but open the other bag," I said while smiling at her scary ass.

"Is it another body part? Cause if so, then nah I'm good. I get the picture crystal fucking clear, Edge," she replied as she shook her head like a damn toddler.

"Man, open the damn bag. It ain't nothing like that," I answered, pushing the smaller bag to her.

I watched as she opened the bag up and pulled out the Tiffany's box. Her eyes grew big as golf balls as she stared at the box and then back to me.

"Will you marry this crazy ass nigga?" I asked her while opening the box revealing the 3-carat princess cut solitaire rose gold ring.

"Yes, Edge, I will marry your crazy ass!" she shouted, pulling me up and kissing me deeply.

I had my girl even though I was damn near ready to send her ass to them pearly gates. I knew I couldn't and that I loved her. This crazy ass nigga was about to be officially off the market, and maybe now I can get my football team of kids. I had the money and was a boss, and now I had a strong woman on my side to hold me down and keep me up on my feet at all times.

23

EGYPT

I had been trying to reach Drip all night because for the third time I was throwing up today and needed his help. I believe I caught a stomach bug from Louve and Kilo's kids after helping out Mrs. Lolly yesterday. She called me and said she had an important meeting at some facility about her son. I remember back when her son and his wife stayed with Mrs. Lolly for a little while, and then the rumors began when her son and family went missing. Rumor was he watched his wife that was pregnant be killed and lost his mind, and he had been checked into a facility since then. Mrs. Lolly had fought to get her grandson and the baby girl who had survived her mother's murder but lost them to the wife's family.

Lately, Mrs. Lolly has been acting weird and secretive about what she has been up to. Yesterday she read the girls a bedtime story, and once they were asleep, I overheard her say great granny loves you to each girl after kissing their forehead. I kept going down the hall to do the laundry for Mrs. Lolly and let it go, but something strange is definitely up. I wasn't feeling too good to try and figure it out now. I needed Drip to take care of me, and his ass was missing in action. I had a feeling he was up to no good, but a bitch was too sick to bother with that. I called Tori but got no answer. That bitch done made up with Edge's crazy ass and got dick silly over there. I couldn't wait to turn up at the wedding.

I dragged myself out of bed and to the shower where I let the hot water soothe me. I got out dried off moisturized my body and threw on a tee and sweats and some fresh all white Ones. I was becoming irritated with Drip's ass and this bullshit. He knew all I asked was to answer when I call and check on me, but he was testing my gangsta to be gone over twenty-four hours and not one call. I hopped in my truck and headed over to the dealership where he sometimes hung out at with Edge or handled business for Edge. I didn't speed there and calmed myself down because I was still feeling a bit nauseous and didn't want to end up throwing up again.

I arrived at the dealership after about twenty minutes of being on the road. I didn't see his truck parked out front, but they sometimes parked around back or at other areas all ride in one car, so I headed inside to see if he was around. I walked in, and the receptionist was on the phone, so I waited for her to finish. It was pretty quiet, so I figured that the guys weren't around. I was tired of waiting and decided just to leave and try Kilo's house.

"I'm sorry about the wait. How may I help you?" she called out to me before I was all the way out of the door.

"I was looking for my boyfriend Drip but he ain't here, so I'm good. Have a nice day," I replied and smiled at her.

"Drip is your man?" she asked with an attitude.

"Yes, he is and always will be, boo" I stated and stepping back inside the door fully giving her the death stare.

"Well, he's been dodging my calls. Maybe you can tell him to call his baby mother." She stood up showing a small pudge in her fitted dress. I almost threw up in my mouth, but I pulled myself together and sucked that shit up.

"Girl bye, that Drip's damn baby? Get the fuck outta here with your thirsty groupie ass. You think we all don't know how you push up and come on to all our men. Better luck next time boo," I replied while smiling in her face keeping my game face on.

I stormed out of there and got in my car. I pulled off letting the tears fall wherever not caring that my vision was getting blurred. I was so sick of this nigga playing me. That bitch may really be pregnant by his ass. Who knows. I was a mess hysterically crying as I sped home. I had no clear view of what was in front of me because the tears took over. Horns were blaring, and I wiped my eyes just in time to see a truck crossing through an intersection. I slammed on my breaks as hard as I could sending my car spinning out of control and slamming into the side of a building.

I was ok just a little shaking up and thank God that the impact of my car hitting the building wasn't as bad as I expected. I climbed out to assess the damage to my car and the building. My car was up on the sidewalk and in the flowers and bushes around the building. I had people coming over asking if I was ok. I advised them I was fine, and I called my insurance company and reported the accident. I waited for a tow truck to arrive to tow my car and give me a lift as well. I was scrolling my phone as I sat on the curb when someone blocked my sun. I looked down at the fresh Jordan Bred ɪɪ's and followed it up into the face of Pras.

I told him all about what caused my accident, and he offered me some encouraging words but told me I had to get myself together and stop letting Dreon take me through all this unnecessary stress. He offered me a ride so that I didn't have to ride with the tow driver. We grabbed some Roscoe's Chicken and Waffles and talked while we ate. I was enjoying my time with Pras. He was mature and laidback and not to mention easy on the eyes. Just as we got in his car, my cell started ringing, and I already knew from the Ella Mai song "Close" that it was Drip. I let it go to voicemail, and he called right back a few more times before shooting me a text to call him.

I ignored all the messages and finished enjoying my time with Pras. I wasn't ready to head home because Drip had started calling from the house phone, and I didn't want to see his face. I let Pras take me to the pool hall where we played pool, had drinks and shot some darts. After I lost count on the drinks, I decided I was done when I felt the room spinning. I felt myself about to throw up, so I ran to the ladies' room and barely made it in a stall before I was throwing up all the contents of my stomach. I felt better after and started to sober up, so I threw some water on my face and headed out. Pras was waiting for me in the hallway. We headed out to his car where to my surprise, I welcomed the kisses and touches he gave. I was sick of Dreon's shit, so tonight I would try to erase him and let Pras make me feel better.

24

KILO

No one had yet to see Louve, and I was sick of the lies Tori was telling for her nappy headed ass bestie. I could hear her ass talking now, and the more I thought about her and the little things I loved, I was missing her more but getting pissed more each day. The girls were missing their mother, and she was calling them always when I was not around, how convenient. KJ was FaceTiming her daily but always acting like he wasn't. Mrs. Lolly was a godsend and had spoken to Louve and switched up on my ass when Louve told her why she left. Now every time I go out, Mrs. Lolly always got a smart ass comment with her old gray hair ass. Like now I know she about to give my ass an earful.

I left early this morning and went to check on some business at the restaurant that Drip and I were working on opening. I walked in, and her ass is right up on the couch waiting for me just as I expected. She looked me up and down and rolled her eyes.

"Is that side part of yours the reason for your early departure out this house?" she asked.

I laughed so hard because she was trying to say sidepiece and said side part. She ain't find shit funny though because she jumped up and was in my face quick as hell.

"Calm down, Mrs. Lolly. I'm behaving myself. Trust me. I was just out handling some business for the restaurant," I replied.

"Yea, well, yo behind gone lose that good woman you got if you keep chasing behind them tots!" she spat as she pointed her finger in my face.

I was trying not to laugh, but she was in here trying to sound like Louve with the words she used, but she was getting them wrong. Louve was all in Mrs. Lolly's ear about me giving her a bad impression of me.

"It's thots, not tots, and no ma'am, I am not chasing no one, but I am on the hunt to find my woman and bring her home where she belongs," I stated and hugged Mrs. Lolly before heading upstairs.

I had to bring my baby home. I missed her ass. I was trying to be patient like Mrs. Lolly advised me after she followed me around the house schooling me as she says. She told me Louve missed and loved me but had to take this time for herself. She broke it down to me how Louve had taken care of people her whole adult life but has been spoiled by all the men around her without having her mother when she needed her the most. Louve was doing some much-needed soul searching to find herself. I completely understood because it was for the better, and she needed that growth. I understood loud and clear, and I was dead ass wrong for the shit I did, and if Louve would just talk to me and come home, she would see that I was sorry and would do whatever I needed to prove it to her.

I decided though after Mrs. Lolly left me to my thoughts that I had enough of waiting to at least see her, so I called up my PI and had him do some research on Louve. I also gave him Mrs. Lolly info so just in case she was secretly meeting up with Louve, he could get the address from her. I needed to go ahead and purchase Louve a ring and stop dragging my feet. I called up the jeweler and made an appointment to discuss designing a ring. From there, I handled a few things that I needed to with the business and made my way to let Naomi down face to face. She had been blowing my phone up for days on end, and it was time to break it to her that this little fling was done.

"Yo Naomi, don't even try to play that game with me ma cause you won't win!" I spat pissed off at the bull shit she was talking.

"Listen, Kilo. I don't know how it happened, but I ain't been with no one but you, and you can be pissed, but I'm keeping my baby," she replied rolling her eyes and snapping her neck like a damn bird.

"No the hell you not!" I shouted and rushed her into the wall snatching her up by the neck.

"Owww! You're hurting me!" she yelled out, clawing at my arms.

"Get a fucking abortion or swim with the fishes, but either way, yo ass ain't keeping shit!" I shouted as I shoved her into the wall a little harder before letting her go.

Naomi dropped to the floor and started sobbing uncontrollably and started to scream and yell that I would pay for the shit I did to her. I had to bounce before I killed this dumb ass girl. I shook my head at her pathetic ass as I headed out the door. I needed a few drinks to get my mind right. The shit I had got myself into was too damn much, so I headed to the bar to drink this shit off.

I was feeling all the shots I threw back, and I knew I needed to get my ass home and in the bed. I left a blue face on the bar and attempted to get up, but the dizziness knocked back down into the bar stool. I rubbed my eyes to focus my vision and then I got up slower this time and made my way to the door. I walked out into the parking lot, and I felt like someone was watching me, but I brushed it off as the liquor. I let the cool breeze sober me up before I got in my car. When I started to feel less dizzy, I hopped in my car and started it up. I still felt that feeling as if someone had eyes on me, and I scanned my surroundings, but nothing seemed out of the ordinary.

I pulled off out the parking space and out the lot heading home to shower and eat. I had a text come in from Louve as I was at the light waiting and I smiled wide as I read her text

Louve Baby: *I'll be coming to the house tomorrow, and I think we need to talk about everything. I love you and miss you Kilo, and you can stop texting me threatening messages. See you tomorrow XOXO*

I read it again and laughed because I had been threatening her ass. I wanted to hear her voice, but I didn't want to push my luck. The light changed, and I pulled off and started my text back to her.

POP, POP, POP, POP!

Gunshots rang out around me, and I swerved over trying to dodge them as they kept coming at my car. I hopped on the highway and realized too late. I was heading in the wrong direction to oncoming traffic when another car swerved over, but we still collided sending my car in the air. All I could do was brace for the impact and pray to the lord to forgive me for my sins before I came to meet him.

SKKKKRRRRTTTTT BOOOOOOOMMMMM!

25

LOUVE

I finished that book and was on to another one but couldn't focus on my book because I kept getting calls from an unknown number, so I stepped outside my mother's room to take the call.

"Hello, I'm looking for the next of kin to a Mr. Kilondre Denton," the caller stated.

"Yes, this is Louve Luxe," I replied nervously.

"We need you to get to the trauma unit of Cedars Sinai Hospital immediately," she explained with urgency.

I hung and headed to the nurse station with tears streaming down my face. Thankfully, I was already at the hospital, and I wanted to tell the nurses where I was headed and let them know I'd be back for my mom. I took the elevator down with my mind racing. I said a prayer for Kilo, and I prayed for the strength to deal with this.

I got down to the trauma and emergency unit, and they gave me the rundown of what happened and what to expect. Kilo was undergoing emergency surgery and needed a blood transfusion. His car was first shot up, he went the wrong way on the highway and then was in an accident. He was hit in the back by two bullets and had a bad head injury and punctured a lung from the accident. I took the test immediately to see if I was a match. I had group texted everyone, and they were all in the waiting area waiting on me to come back out. Mrs. Lolly even came with the kids and prayed with us and over us. I was on pins and needles as I sat and waited. I couldn't believe this was happening. My ass was away all this time, and this is what I come back to.

Edge was pacing back and forth, and I made Tori keep her eye on him because I knew he would try to go out and do some stupid, reckless ass shit that we didn't need. Tori was a mess and tried to hold it together for me, but we were all a family, so it was hard on us all. We were all we had. Drip was losing it, and he couldn't reach Egypt, and that had him tripping hard. He was waiting on word about Kilo, but I told him to go find Egypt and check on her because none of us had heard from her at all today. I was worried about everyone right about now because it's no telling what the hell these guys have been out here doing to have this type shit happen.

I pleaded with Drip, and he finally went to look for Egypt just as the doctors came back and told me that I wasn't a match. Everyone lined up to try and be a match, and that warmed my hurting heart. As time passed on, they said each of us wasn't a match, and we were running out of time. I had no clue what we were going to do, but Mrs. Lollly stood up and offered to try.

"I believe I may be a match because Kilondre is my paternal grandson," she said, letting tears drop as her lip quivered.

"What are you saying? Mrs. Lolly, what is going on?" I said in disbelief.

"I had been conducting some research to verify, and when I took my son who is a mental facility a picture of Kilondre, he said that was his son. See Kilondre's mother went to jail for killing my son's wife. They were in a love triangle gone wrong. My son, Killon Brinks, was a big man out in the streets at this time in the early '80s, and he had women all over him, but his wife Tracy was his boss' daughter. That's why he married her and was in love with Kilondre's mother, Kima. Tracy tried to Kill Killon for trying to leave her for Kilondre's mother and his son. Kima saved Killon's life by killing Tracy before she could kill him. Kima went to jail for this, and Tracy's father made sure she got long, hard time from his connections in the system. Killon was told that Kima was killed in jail, and he lost his mind. All this time we were told Tracy's family killed Kilondre, but when I came to interview for the nanny position and seen Kilo, I knew he was my grandson. I didn't know how to tell him and was waiting for the right time, but if I am a match and can save my grandson's life, then I had to let it be known," she said, sobbing.

I was at a loss for words and just grabbed her and hugged her tightly. They led her back to see if she was a match, and we all sat and waited again. I needed to tell Edge about our mother but now wasn't the time. I would wait until everything had been settled and Kilo was in recovery because my baby was gone pull through. I had faith. No matter how hard it was, I had to keep the faith. I held my babies as well waited, and I rubbed my belly for the one growing in there. Our family wasn't complete without Kilo, and I wanted no life without my soul mate.

26

DRIP

I had called Egypt so much and left so many voicemails her mailbox was now full. I know she was mad as hell at me, but right now was important, and I needed to know she was ok. I know she was thinking that I was out here doing her dirty, but I wasn't. I was tied up with that shit we had to do with Saga and getting shit cleared up with the Dons. I went to our house, and her car wasn't there. I then remembered that I had put the GPS tracker on her car, so I logged in and pressed the locate button. I plugged the location in my car and was on my way to wherever she was at.

I was far as hell out the way from where we lived, damn near in Hollywood. I pulled up to the address, and it was nice ass townhome. I sat and contemplated a few possible scenarios and how I should react and handle this shit. I was cool as hell and about to just ring the bell and see what was up because it could be a coworker's home and not no nigga like my mind was yelling at me that it was. I parked right in front of the driveway blocking her car in because if it was some foul shit, I know how Egypt gets. She'll try to run off, but not today. I was almost out the driveway when I doubled back to the car.

This was the same car I saw her ass get out of in front of that restaurant with that nigga Pras before. I walked around the car to check the license plate, praying with each step that it wouldn't be the plate, but no such luck. The Lord has been stopped answering my prayers with my fucked-up ass ways, so I ain't surprise. It was that nigga Pras' car as expected.

I stormed to the door and started beating that bitch down. It took about five minutes before anyone came to the door. That nigga peeped out the window blinds, and we made eye contact, and then I assumed he walked away. He never opened the door, and that pissed me off more, so I started kicking that shit trying to break it in. I jumped off the porch and ran to my car to get my gun. I was done playing nice with this nigga, and Egypt knew how crazy I was, so I guess that's why she came running out the house looking like she just woke up. She had on some leggings and an oversized tee. I closed my eyes and counted to ten because of the shit I was already feeling behind Kilo, and now this was about to send me off the edge.

"Dreon, what is your problem? You can't come here acting like this!" she shouted, stomping her feet and throwing her hands up to her head when I pulled my bat out my trunk.

"Kill all that noise because you know me, Egypt! This is me Drip, and you know how I go when it comes to you. Yo, what the fuck are you doing at this clown's house?" I yelled as I ran up on her and sandwiched her on the trunk of her car.

"Yo, back up off her, homie," Pras said, trying to step up in between us. I dropped the bat and delivered a right hook to his jaw sending him to the ground cradling his face like a bitch.

"Is this the nigga you choosing?" I screamed letting spit fly out like a maniac. I was way past my limit, and Egypt looked terrified.

"Nigga, fuck you! That's why when your bitch needed someone I was there with a shoulder to cry and dick to ride on!" Pras shouted still holding his jaw and standing to his feet.

I was ready to charge at him, but Egypt pushed me back hard as hell causing me to flex at her ass, and she jumped back quick in fear.

"Oh, you protecting this nigga? Tell me Egypt did you fuck him?" I yelled, stepping back into her face.

"YOU DON'T LIKE IT, DO IT? I WAS SICK AS A DOG AND ALL

I WANTED SHIT ALL I NEEDED WAS YOU, AND YET YOU
DIDN'T COME HOME, AND I COULDN'T GET IN TOUCH WITH
YOU. I DROVE TO ALL THE PLACES THAT I FIGURED YOU'D
BE, INCLUDING THE DEALERSHIP DRIP AND THAT BITCH ASS
RECEPTIONIST TOLD ME SHE PREGNANT BY YOU, NIGGA. I
HAVE FORGAVE YOU TIME AND TIME AGAIN DRIP, AND YOU
PROMISE THAT YOU'LL CHANGE! YO ASS IS A LIE! YOU AIN'T
NEVER GONE CHANGE. SHIT DON'T FEEL GOOD TO HAVE
YOUR HEART CRUSHED, HUH?" she yelled at the top of her lungs,
crushing me with each word.

"So that's the type time you on right now, E? Damn, not my Egypt
yo. I can't even deal with this shit. Our family is laid up in the hospital
fighting for his life, and you out here being a hoe on some spiteful get
back shit. You flaw as fuck for that bogus ass shit, but I'm a let you
rock how you want you got it though, E."

I threw her the deuces and hopped in my ride. She came running
to my car banging on the window, yelling for me to wait, but I was
good on her and this bullshit. Fuck that.

"That bitch is lying too. I hope that lie was worth it, and that
revenge dick was good to you," I said through the window I had
rolled down before pulling off. I could see her yelling up in Pras' face
and then hopping in her car and coming down the street behind me
heading in the same direction that I was driving in.

27

EDGE

I was racking my brain trying to find out who would do this shit to Kilo. I had some of my people out trying to gather information. I was also trying to keep Tori calm because she was stressing that the shit I'd done to Saga's bitch ass was the cause of all this. I was sick seeing my sister so broken up and hurt, and trying to console her was hard. Mrs. Lolly ended up being a match, and I knew that things were gone turn out good for my boy. I pulled Kilo back into this life so that he could level up and be good. We had our hands in the streets, but we had legit businesses, so we weren't out here just for nothing.

I started to think about all the times I lied to Louve about what I did solely for income. I had started a storm of bullshit with my lies trying to protect my sister. I had a father in jail fighting to get a twenty-five-year sentence reduced and a fucked mother out here living her life on drugs on the street. I had so much pain, and anger built up for the way my mom left us and let drugs be more important than her family. She was the honest reason why I was scared to commit fully, but Tori was it for me, and now we had a wedding to plan and get ready for.

I wanted kids and a wife to come home time, and at thirty-five, I wasn't getting no younger. I loved the way Tori loved my family and me with no ill intentions. She held me down and pushed me to do better and be better. We meshed with little problems, and the few we had, was usually my fault for dealing with these bum ass girls out here.

Looking around the waiting room, I realized the severity of this shit for real. We were camped out waiting for the outcome of the blood transfusion and surgery that Kilo was having. That could be me in there right now, and life was too short to live watching over your shoulder.

Louve kept going to the reception desk and whispering to the nurse, and I was starting to get worried that shit was bad with Kilo, and she was hiding it. I waited as she spoke to another nurse or aide and then came back over to where we all were camped out at in the waiting room. She sat down nervously bouncing her leg and biting her nails. I got up and went over to where she was sitting. I pulled her close and hugged her to let her know I was here, and she wasn't in this alone. I had never seen Louve like this, and not being able to make it better for her like I have done all the times she needed me to do, was killing me. I was about to ask Louve what the nurses were saying and what they were discussing, but the nurse rushed over before I could speak.

"Ms. Luxe your mother is awake, and I told her how you had been here waiting for her to awake all week. She broke down crying and asked for me to get you," the nurse stated without stopping to take a breath.

"Wait. Hold up. Louve, what is this lady talking about your mom? Is she talking about *our* mom?" I questioned Louve intensely.

"I'm sorry that you had to find out like this Edge, but daddy knew you wouldn't want to help mom, so he sent me to find her and help. When I went to where Uncle Vern said she had been staying, I was sent here because she was in a medically induced coma," she replied, wiping away some tears.

I didn't know what to say, but Louve grabbed my hand and led me to the elevator. I was in shock and at a loss for words while also being mad that no one told me. My pops had just talked to me this morning and never mentioned shit. I saw Uncle Vern yesterday, and Louve could have easily told me and let me in in this. During the elevator ride, I felt like the same little boy that I was when our mother left us for good. We got off the elevator and reached the room, but we stood outside, and Louve blocked the entrance.

"Edge she is still our beautiful mother, but she has lost a lot of weight and hair, and she looks like a zombie," she warned.

"It's cool, Louve, I won't be rude or judge her. I'ma act cool and like I have some sense left. Hahaha, but for real, this shit that we are going through with Kilo has me looking at a lot of things differently. Life is too short LouLou," I stated, kissing her forehead.

We walked in the room, but it was empty, and all our mothers' things were gone. I locked eyes with Louve, and we knew she had left and was back out in the streets. I felt like that kid again getting excited to see a mother you love but is she never around. Louve broke down in tears, and all I could do was hold my sister. Today was a rough ass day and the night wasn't even over yet.

To Be Continued

SNEAK PEEK

A Dopeboy's Trash A Plug's Treasure
TREASURE

I had stayed up twenty-four hours straight because my mind was racing, and my heart was hurting. I know it's partly my fault that I am hurting, but Shyne promised me that last time was the last time that he'd do me like this. I moved all the way out here to Miami with him while he chased his dope boy dreams. I had no one close here to confide in except my neighbor Sparkle. She was cool, but she never wanted to go out or do anything. We were young and in Miami, the party city, but hardly went to the beach let alone a party. My mother told me not to leave with this nigga, but at twenty, I thought I was grown and had found the love of my life. Shyne treated me good for the first two years, and there wasn't a soul that could tell me he didn't love me. But here we were five years into it, and I didn't know who he even was anymore. He wasn't coming home at night anymore, sometimes days in a row, and I knew then that he had to be cheating because we don't know many people out here. And he wasn't sleeping in the trap that I knew for a fact from the multiple times I popped up there, and he was nowhere to be found.

Tonight I had no energy to go looking for him though. I honestly wanted out of this one-sided relationship and now was the time to break free while he was laid up with God knows who. I could make a dash for it and never look back. I was tired of the lies, the private phone calls, and the vandalizing of my car more times than I can count. Who was I kidding? I wasn't going anywhere. Shit, I couldn't go anywhere. I ain't have nowhere to go yet, and I refused to move back home.

I didn't have anything of my own to get up and leave with, and for that reason, I was stuck where I was because I let a man provide and control me. Today I was deciding to set myself up in a position to leave and do for myself. There wasn't any love left in this house, and I was starting to think there never really was. Shyne hadn't touched me in weeks let alone made love to me in years. It was a time that he couldn't keep his hands off me, and I never felt lonely. The sad truth is he always was a rude ass nigga though, but my silly, young and dumb ass loved it back then.

I got out my laptop and started researching culinary schools. I always loved cooking and baking so what better time than now to go to school and start my dream career. I wanted a catering business restaurant, bar, and bakery. Today was the first day of the rest of my life. I decided to focus this time and energy that I waste crying and hurting over Shyne into building my myself up and over. I sent a text to Sparkle to see if she wanted to help me research schools that I found for culinary in the area, and she said she was down, so I decided to get dressed and start my day off more positive despite this nigga making my life negative and draining. As of today, it's fuck Shyne. It's all about Treasure from here on out.

Had I listened I wouldn't be in this situation, but they say everything happens for a reason, so I'd take this as the path I was supposed to be on and focus on me for once. Shyne had shown me that you can't become attached and reliant on anyone, even if they claim to love you and you promise to always take care of you because that can change without any notice or warning. Shyne did exactly that and worse to me with no rhyme or reason why, and I could no longer sit by and wait for him to change when it was obvious that he never would. I'd learned a lesson the hard and hurtful way. I cried and asked why he was treating me the way he was, and I had now reached the point where I was praying for God to remove my pain and hurt and help me get over him, and I woke up today different after that prayer. It hurt, but nothing like how it hurt before. I knew the time had finally come to move on and make Treasure happy.

Sparkle

I decided to pull my hair back into a tight ponytail and get ready to workout. Working out was a way to relieve stress, especially since I was celibate and backed up going through a drought. I was starting to get used to the nice weather in Miami, and I couldn't wait to feel comfortable enough to go out and enjoy it, besides the small patio I sat on at times. I had been in Miami for six months now after I had to pack up for the third time and leave everything behind. I ran off almost two years ago from my abusive ex-husband, and when a friend of his ran into me, I had to pick up and leave before he found out it was me and my secret would be revealed. Almost two years ago, I faked my death and started a new identity. If Goose knew I was still alive, he would surely kill my ass for real this time.

I met Goose when I was sixteen working as a lookout girl for a local drug dealer in our neighborhood. My mother was sick. She had a terminal illness, and I had to provide for us. My father was in jail serving twenty years for killing the man who killed his mother. They called it a crime of passion and diagnosed my father with mental illness. He would be home in a few years, and I know he was looking for me once the money and letters stopped coming and my number changed. When my mother died, Goose was my shoulder to cry on. He helped me get my first place, which became our first place, and soon we were a couple. He made me stop hustling, and I went to school and got my degree as a pharmacist, but he never let me work to use it.

I thought I had the perfect man until Goose became possessive and violent with me. As time went on it only got worse, and as my young body developed, he began to really trip over anything I wore and anywhere I tried to go. It got to the point where all I did was sit in the house depressed and ready to end it all. One day, I watched a Lifetime movie and got the idea to fake my death. I was able to convince Goose to let me work part-time because I was too bored. I used the time wisely and didn't really work part-time but per diem at the local CVS. I retrieved a dummy mannequin and started my plan.

One night I told him I was called in for a late shift and my plan was set in motion. I drove my car close by work off the freeway where I had paid a crack head to crash into my car for two hundred dollars. After he left the scene, I set the mannequin dressed like me and the one dressed like an older lady in the other car. I had spent good money ordering these life-like dolls on the black web. I dressed the doll in my pharmacy coat and badge, and I made sure my identical lace front was on there as well. I put the wedding rings and the jewelry and my purse and cell phone in the car as well. I poured gas over the two crashed vehicles and tossed a match before I hightailed it with a book bag, new identity, and a new cellphone.

I had a bus ticket under my new name Sparkle Reynolds, and I was never looking back. That was almost two years ago, and so far, no one here in Miami knew a thing. I only talked to my neighbor Treasure and my therapist because I suffered bad with depression and paranoia. I felt like any day he would come and find me.

I was just finishing with doing my home workout in my spare room that I had made a gym when there was a knock at my door. Out of habit, I retrieved my gun from my hiding spot in my closet and placed it in the small of my back. I crept to the door and checked through the peephole. I was instantly relieved when I saw my friend and neighbor Treasure on the other side of my door. I relaxed and opened the door up, and Treasure smiling brightly pranced right in like a runway model. She was carrying a box of cannolis from the bakery in our building and a glass pitcher of her homemade mimosa punch that has become my favorite Sunday pick me up.

We never hung out anywhere other than each other's apartments, the gym in our building, and at the pool. That was all my doing as I didn't want to risk being seen by anyone that knew Goose. As I mentioned, I suffered bad with paranoia and really hoped that one day this all would pass so that I could live my life not confined to my home. Surprisingly though, Treasure never pressured me for us to go out. I grabbed the box of cannolis from her and headed to the couch. I turned off the workout video and turned on *The Real* talk show. Treasure poured us some glasses of the mimosa punch and joined me in the living room on the couch. We talked and laughed about everything for almost an hour or so before she started to tell me the story about what Shyne had done this damn time.

"Sparkle, I am putting my plan in place. As of today, I will be moving on. I have to leave this nigga alone before he drives me absolutely insane. I can't keep doing these drive-bys to his trap spots and pulling up at the club acting a whole fool and a half out here. Nah, I'm over that shit. I got me a nice little amount of money saved up, so I will be getting me a place tucked off where he doesn't know where it is, and I'ma change my number and just ghost his ass. I promise that because I can't do this shit no more man." She blew air in frustration as she wiped the tears from her eyes. I passed her the box of Kleenex.

I knew Treasure's pain all too well and a pain that was far much worse than this. I'm a 100% certain that what I endured with Goose was more than enough to drive any woman crazy. Shit, it pushed me to fake my death because I knew death was my only way out, and Goose told me that on the daily. Starting over was the best thing I could have ever done, but that was a gift and a curse. I literally still live each day in fear of Goose. I worry that he will find me and really kill me, and I hated this fear shit with a passion.

I rubbed Treasure's back and decided to throw caution to the wind. I decided we needed to go out. I had to live my life, and that started today because Treasure needed to live too.

"Girl, fuck Shyne's cheating ass. Let's go out and enjoy Miami," I said, shocking her and my damn self.

"Oh my god, really? Little quiet Miss Sparkle is down to go out to the club and party?" She shouted hopping up from the couch pulling me up with her and hugging me tightly.

"Let's go shopping, get our hair and nails done, and let's turn up tonight because come tomorrow, I will be apartment shopping and packing, and you can help me," she rambled on nonstop, and I just laughed at her extra ass.

We got ready and hit the mall up where we shopped and pampered ourselves for hours before we finally left grabbing some Chick-fil-A on our way back to my apartment. By nine p.m., we were snapping pictures for Snapchat, Facebook, and the Gram. We called up an Uber so that we could get lit tonight.

We decided to hit up Club Luxe Grand. It was a nice upscale club that had one of the dopest DJs and two huge dancefloors on each level. We were in our own VIP section just vibing, drinking, and doing our own thing. I was on cloud nine having the time of my life with my best friend, and no one or anything could ruin that. I may have found our new past time for Treasure and me to let loose and be free.

I was on my third drink, and Treasure was probably on her fifth. She was standing up on the sofa in our section winding her hips the Reggae beat, and I was seated sitting pretty dancing in my seat. I was just standing up when Treasure jumped down brushing past me fast, damn near knocking me over and causing my drink to spill. I threw back the rest of my 1738 and followed behind the raging bull she had morphed, into storming off through the crowd. I rushed to catch up to her, but I wasn't fast enough because just as I reached her, she had thrown her drink in Shyne's face. We were diagonal across from our section in another larger section that Shyne was posted in standing off to the side with a chick in his lap. The girl jumped up soaked from head to breasts in 1738 screaming and stomping like a child. Everything happened so fast from there that I didn't even see him yoke Treasure up until he had her in the air by her neck.

I was trying my hardest to release his hand from around her throat. As I struggled to pry his hands off Treasure, she kicked and clawed at him drawing blood from his wrist. Security rushed up on us and helped separate everyone. Two guards pulled us one way, and one guard shoved Shyne the opposite direction towards the back of the club. The guards escorted us out the club and to the parking lot where they watched us as we waited on the Uber. Treasure was pissed off and had been going off the whole time we had been waiting for the Uber.

Although things ended abruptly, I still had a good time and an eventful night thanks to my front row seats at The Treasure and Shyne show. I was still feeling good off the liquor and getting a kick out of Treasure still going off on a rant.

"What the hell are you smiling for, Sparkle? This shit ain't even funny man. I'm so pissed right now!" she yelled and stomped her feet crossing her arms over her chest pulling me from my thoughts.

"Calm down, Mike Tyson! Just relax girl damn, and it actually is very funny. Treasure, sis, we gone laugh at this damn night one day soon and then we'll be able to laugh about it FOREVVVVA (in my Cardi B voice)!" I said laughing with tears just as the Uber pulled into the lot. Treasure rolled her eyes but burst out laughing right along with me.

Shyne

I was hot as fuck right about now behind Treasure's big head ass. This girl done came up in the VIP section that I had for my team and some potential ruthless ass little niggas I needed as my hittas because they were official with their hit rate never missing a target. I was building my team up, and they were the missing piece I needed especially to show Honour that I should be the next distro for his new territory. I was trying to gain their respect and show them how good we were living over here to bait them into joining our team. This damn girl done showed her ass and showed out for real, and I was ready to smack her ass upside her head, but security saved her silly ass.

Not to mention, I had this sexy little Haitian chick that I was trying to get to roll with me to the telly, but after Treasure ruined her dress and her made lace front lift, the bitch got ghost on a nigga. I had the right mind to head around to the front of the club and find Treasure so that I could smack some sense into her. I hadn't been home in a few days, and I wasn't taking her calls, but that don't matter I'm the man of the house I do as I please. All she needs to do is sit pretty, spend my money, and take care of a nigga. Regardless of what I do, she supposed to act accordingly, carry herself better, and hold that shit down.

My side chick Rori was starting to take up all my time, and juggling her with Treasure was becoming a task. Quite frankly I felt like ditching Treasure ass and putting Rori in her spot. Rori had been around now for damn near a year, and I had no plans of letting her go. She had the best wet wet I've ever had, and her head was official. I originally met Rori on some business shit, but she was feeling the kid from day one, and things started up and never stopped. Rori was a self-made boss, and the only female in Miami owning and operating a successful luxury car dealership. She was known to hook top dealers up with fly rides, but I had a business idea that proved to be lucrative for her and me and we been rocking since then.

Rori knew all about Treasure and made it a point to tell me to leave her alone and come be with her. I was really considering doing just that, but I felt obligated to Treasure since I moved her far away from her family and friends back home to follow my dope boy ambitions. I came to Miami two years ago after my nigga Roman had to go take a time out and sit tight for a couple of years. He put me in contact with his peoples Honour the HNIC out here in Miami, and his reach went to damn near every state in the south. Roman told me that if I wanted to make some real paper, then I needed to link up with Honour, put in that work, make them major moves, and I'd be straight.

I wasn't a true boss just yet, but I was damn near there, and I that knew once I secured the rest of my team, we would be so thorough that Honour would have no choice but to really put me on and give me a higher position. The money was flowing in, everyone was eating, and all violators were always handled and checked immediately. I was also able to provide and spoil Treasure. I had been slacking lately but the truth is I loved Treasure, but I was feeling Rori too. The shit would be dope if they would agree to do the sister wives shit, but hey, I guess bitches had standards and shit or whatever.

I owed Treasure to take care of her and give her anything she wanted, and for a while, I did just that, but I'm a man, and Miami got some bad females. Treasure had held shit down a few times when I was just nickel and diming and pushing real light work. She was down for me and loved me when I ain't have shit but a twin bed in my momma's basement. I knew when she followed me here that I had to keep her. Shit, I had planned on marrying her ass and having a few babies, but that all came to a standstill when Rori popped on the scene. I had two chicks that were willing to ride, and each gave me something the other couldn't.

Treasure was beautiful, but Rori was a bad chick. Rori reminded me of Jessica Dime from *Love & Hip Hop Atlanta*. Rori was down for me and was a true team player. Treasure was always on me about leaving the game and starting a legit business. Treasure was ready for marriage and kids, and in the beginning, I wanted to give her just that, but Rori was down for the threesome's party life and getting to the money. Rori was my Bonnie in the streets and a certified freak in the sheets. I knew sooner rather than later I'd either have to give them both an ultimatum just to deal how we are or let one go.

Rori somedays had me ready to drop Treasure, but then I remembered that she couldn't cook, and she doesn't clean shit she hires maids. That alone in my eyes was a red flag that she was not wife material and couldn't birth my kids at all. Treasure, on the other hand, was exactly that— the perfect wife and would be the perfect mother for my kids. She cooked, cleaned, and rubbed a nigga down at the end of the day all that. However, here lately, she's been nagging me making me stay away from her because she was irritating. I know if I didn't get shit together, Treasure would for sure pack up and go back to Charlotte.

I left the club after smoking a few blunts to calm myself before I deal with Treasure. Tonight was perfect because Rori was in Vegas looking into expanding her dealership, so she wouldn't be home until tomorrow. I knew Treasure was gone be on good bullshit once I got in the house, so I mentally prepared myself for a showdown, and then I'd dick her down properly like always maybe put a seed up in her to keep her ass under lock. Just before I reached the exit for our condo of the highway, I had a picture message come in from Rori and that caused me to pass by my exit and keep going to hers.

Rori was back early and dressed in nothing but a thong and heels, and I wasn't passing her ass up now. I'd give Treasure a minute to cool off and head home in a few hours. I knew once I got in Rori's that I'd have to power my phone off because Treasure was gone be blowing my line up. I must of spoke too soon because the phone started to vibrate in the cup holder of my Range, and the media display said the incoming call was from boss man A.K.A Honour. I already knew why he was calling, and he was probably pissed, so I let it roll to the voice-mail. I know he got some shit to say about me pistol whooping Javier, but he crossed the line and was talking reckless, and I had to prove my point someway somehow. Right now, Rori was clouding my better judgement, and oh well, I'd hit him back later.

Honour

I was laughing to myself to keep from spazzing out because this nigga had to take me for a damn joke. I was running out of patience for this nigga Shyne. I only looked out for him on the strength of my cousin Roman from Charlotte, NC. Roman was pushing heavy weight for me down there, and he said he wouldn't have been able to do it without his partner Shyne. Roman knows how I get down, so if I took on a referral that I didn't know personally then I must really respect, love or fuck with you heavy.

When Roman took the plea deal on a bullshit gun charge, he sent

Shyne my way. Now, in the beginning, he was on point and thorough. But, here we are two years later, and this nigga was feeling himself and was slacking with work. He was carrying on day to day like he was a boss out here making executive decisions without being given the directive to do so. I was calling this nigga for an emergency meeting because the pistol whooping that he decided to give Javier backfired on his ass in a major way. Javier was so mad that he snatched up all the money, drugs, and guns from one of the top traps and attempted to split town. He shot a little nigga in the leg that worked at the trap that tried to stop him before he dipped out of there.

I had my right hand goon ass little cousins Cairo and Pharaoh on his ass though. He thought he was about to get away, but they were waiting for the right time to snatch his ass up. Them little niggas loved the element of surprise when they had to put in work on some niggas or do a hit. This whole situation was all on Shyne, and this nigga had the nerve to not be answering the phone. I decided to go to his condo he thought I knew nothing about. I hopped in my red McLaren 540c Coupe and hit the pedal to the metal over there. Twenty minutes tops, and I was pulling into the parking lot of the Coral Gables luxury condos.

I had a little cutie that stayed in these same condos, so I hit her up and asked her to let me in the building. She made me promise to stop up at her condo and see her once I finished whatever business I had to handle. I promised, but I never said tonight, and I guess she'd figure it out when I never showed up, but I didn't care I was on a mission right now.

Once she buzzed me in the doors, I went right to the unit listing for mail to locate his unit number. I scanned over the mailbox directory until I came to Shyne's country bumpkin ass last name, Blumford, with a second name, Belmont, listed as well. I had no clue who name that was because his chick Rori had a big ass house somewhere far out, and her last name was Diaz. This nigga Shyne probably had a country ass chick up in this spot that he kept hidden from everyone. I wonder if Rori knew what this nigga was about, but knowing her, she probably does know and just doesn't give a fuck. She's a shallow broad, bad or not she is weak as fuck.

I rode the elevator up to the sixth floor. I checked myself out on some G shit in the elevator mirrors cause a nigga was handsome, and I always stayed fresh as fuck. I was dressed casually, real laid back and chill, in my Nike jogger suit with the matching black Jordan retro 12's. As I was getting off and heading around the corner, I could hear a woman cursing loudly and going off at the mouth. As soon as I turned the corner, my eyes fell upon a beautiful woman tossing clothes of what I assume was a nigga's shit out the door into the hall. I assumed she was the loud talker I had heard when I first stepped off the elevator.

I checked my Bulova watch and realized it was well after four in the morning and was surprised that security hadn't been called yet on her. As I headed down the hall towards her, I realized that it was Shyne's apartment that she was going in and out of throwing clothes and items from. I walked right up to the door that had just closed behind her perfect round bottom in leggings and a sports bra. I waited off to the side after stepping over the mountain of items on the floor of the hallway. I could hear her going off still, but I didn't hear Shyne or anyone else saying anything.

She swung the door open and froze in place as ours met and locked on each other. I was frozen speechless in my place against the wall posted up. I was captivated by her beauty, and her presence gave me a high.

"I'm sorry can I help you with something?" she asked as she broke our intense stare and dropped the clothes into the pile.

"My bad, beautiful, I was looking for Shyne. Is he home?" I asked never breaking eye contact with her. She huffed and rolled her eyes at the mention of his name which made me smile.

"Fuck Shyne. He ain't here, and as you can see, he won't be here other than to pick this shit up!" she shouted as she did an about turn in furry UGG house slippers and storming back into the apartment.

I followed her inside and shut the door behind me. I walked into more shit scattered and thrown about around the apartment. She was nowhere to be found in the living room, so I assumed she had wandered to the back of the apartment. I had a seat at the bar and poured me a shot of D'usse. She stormed back out and screamed grabbing her chest upon seeing me seated in her bar stools posted up with a shot that I went ahead and threw back. I winked at her, and she rolled her eyes.

"Why are you all up in my house just helping yourself to whatever? That is just rude as fuck to invite yourself into someone's home, and you didn't even introduce your damn self," she said angrily with her hand propped up on her hip, and her other hand positioned as if to say *what the fuck* like the memes that be going around. I couldn't help but laugh at her feisty little ass.

"My bad, shorty. My name is Honour, and I'm Shyne's boss. It's imperative that I speak to him, so I decided to wait around," I replied as I stood to my feet and extended my hand to shake hers but was interrupted by the ringing of my cell phone. Checking the caller ID, I saw that it was my right hand, my cousin, Pharaoh calling me. I answered on the next ring right away to see what was good.

"Yo P, what's good?" I asked still watching lil mama watch me.

"Big cuz, we got a problem. Where are you at right now so that I can come to you? This is major, and I don't usually do the whole emergency thing with you, and you know that, but this shit is deep and requires your immediate attention, boss man," he said, sounding defeated and worried which caused me to be alarmed.

"Aight well, I'm at Shyne's crib right now. I tried to pull up on him in person since he wasn't answering my calls and texts, but he ain't here. Just his girl is here," I said, walking over to the bar to get another shot.

"Whoa nigga, you and shorty better get up outta there right now. We pulled the recording of Javier's car, and he's a rat. That nigga talking to the FEDS right now as we speak and he gone be sending them over Shyne's way. They are rounding up a team and coming to Shyne's condo out in Coral Gables, so if that's the location you at, I suggest you hightail it up outta there. You don't want none of the problems that they about to bring Shyne's way. Bro, dip now, I'm out."

He disconnected the call, and I was stuck as to what the fuck was going on in my camp.

My first thought was just to dip out immediately, but I felt like I couldn't leave shorty here to be tied up in Shyne's mess.

"Yo, your man got some heat from the FEDS. They're coming here any minute, so I suggest you leave now like I'm about to do. If you need a ride, come on shorty, let me know where to take you. I'd feel better knowing you're not left behind and tied up in this shit," I said as I stood in the window and checked the parking lot

"What? OMG! I could kill this nigga! He fucking promised. Damn it, Treasure, think... think. Shit, I don't have anyone other than my neighbor Sparkle, and I don't want to impose on her or wrap her in this shit either." She was talking fast as she paced back and forth running her hands through her hair.

"Baby girl, I know you don't know my rude ass at all, but I'ma be rolling out that door in the next minute, and if you are rolling, then let's go, but either way, I'm out," I said before heading towards the front door.

Once at the door, I stopped and looked behind me to see her dash off to the back. I just shook my head as I went out the door assuming she was staying there. All I could do was hope baby girl didn't get caught up in his mess.

"Hey, rude ass, wait up a damn minute. I didn't say I wasn't coming with you!" she yelled, running to catch up with me. She dragged her rolling luggage and a duffle bag over one shoulder and had a purse in her other hand.

I just smiled at her as I held the elevator door open for her. Once on the elevator, we stood in silence. I was about to speak until the muffled barking noises erupted through the silenced elevator ride. I looked to her confused with a brow raised waiting for an explanation. She smiled back at me nervously and unzipped the duffle bag pulling out a fluffy dog with big pink hair bows on each ear and a pink dog collar. All I could do was laugh and shake my head as I grabbed her rolling luggage as we got off the elevator. We headed through the lobby right out the front to my McLaren. I placed her bags in the trunk, and she sat holding her puppy in her lap in my front seat. I hopped in, started up the car, blasting Future's "March Madness" as we pulled out of the lot.

As we left the lot, a swarm of unmarked police cars was pulling up in the parking lot, and we both shook our heads in disbelief at how close we were to being right in the condo as they arrived. I don't know what I was thinking by snatching up and helping out Ms. Treasure, but I was liking her presence and vibe right now. She was having an effect on me.

COMING SOON...

L. Renee Catalog
Losing Lyric
Once Upon A Hood Love: A Brooklyn Fairytale
I'll Be Home For Christmas: A Holiday Novella

CPSIA information can be obtained
at www.ICGtesting.com
Printed in the USA
LVHW041544090519
617264LV00003B/463